From the Files of

Madison Finn

Read all the books about Madison Finn!

Coming Soon!

Don't miss the Super Edition

From the Files of
Madison Finn

Keep It Real

By Laura Dower

HYPERION
New York

To Rich, Myles, and Olivia
for keeping me real all the time

Text copyright © 2005 by Laura Dower

From the Files of Madison Finn and the Volo colophon are trademarks of Disney Enterprises, Inc.
Volo® is a registered trademark of Disney Enterprises, Inc.

Printed in the United States of America

First Edition
1 3 5 7 9 10 8 6 4 2

The main body of text of this book is set in 13-point Frutiger Roman.

ISBN 0-7868-5687-4

Visit www.hyperionbooksforchildren.com

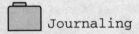 Journaling

Rude Awakening: For once, homework isn't going to be a piece of cake--it's going to be the WHOLE cake.

Just when I think I'm getting behind in my school work, I get a killer assignment that just about GUARANTEES me an A (or maybe an A+, fingers *so* crossed) in Mr. Gibbons's English class. It's like someone just handed me the golden ticket in Willy Wonka.

We started "journaling," which is basically keeping track of feelings and observations and all that . . . which is what I do every day on this computer anyway! I think it's great that everyone else in school is going to discover just

how great it can be to keep files like I
do. In journaling we have to write in a
composition notebook. That's the only
difference.

Apparently, we have some assessment
tests coming up later this year, so Mr.
Gibbons says we all need to get more
comfortable--and more skilled--with our
writing. All the English sections in the
seventh grade are doing this, so Fiona,
Aimee, Lindsay, and I are already planning
times when we can write together, like
afternoons at Aimee's dad's Cyber Cafe.
Mom says it sounds like we want to do what
people did a long time ago in sewing
circles. Talk about a time warp. Imagine us
a hundred or two hundred years ago sitting
around making a quilt?

Madison fingered the pages of the brand-new
black-and-white composition notebook sitting on
top of the desk in her room. She and Mom had
picked it up at the stationery store after school that
day. She eyed a pink sheet of paper tacked up on her
bulletin board. The first journaling assignment was
due in the morning, and she hardly knew where to
begin. She read over the handout Mr. Gibbons had
given the class.

Journaling #1
Mode: Narrative
Planning: Make a list of events you plan to use in

your story. Events are usually told in chrono-
logical order.
Focus: Start a story with a quote or action. Get
the reader's attention right away.
Topic: Write a story about yourself that details a
moment at school. It can be a moment of
success or an embarrassing moment.

Madison gnawed on the end of her fat purple
pencil and leaned over her favorite doodle pad (the
one with the picture of a pug just like her dog, Phin).
Naturally, she wanted to write a story about success.
Who would ever choose to write about an embarrassing moment?

Madison scoured her memory bank. In third
grade, she had been elected president of her class in
a landslide vote. Did that moment of success count?
It seemed like such a long time ago—long before she
had had a falling out with her classmate (and now
mortal enemy) Ivy Daly, otherwise known as "Poison
Ivy"; before Hart Jones (her übercrush) had left
school for the first time; and before her newest BFF,
Fiona Waters, had moved to Far Hills from California.

Should she write the story of winning the elec-
tion? Or should she write about helping Mrs. Wing
design the school Web page? Or participating in a
sold-out fifth-grade concert as the principal flute
player? Which one sounded the best? Madison wanted
to pick something that seemed impressive. After all,

while no one read her files, someone else *would* be reading *these* stories.

Phin arched his back and let out a little squeal, the noise he always made whenever he stretched and yawned at the same time. Madison turned away from her desk to pick him up. He needed a bath, Madison thought as she nuzzled his ears. He also needed her to clean out his little pug nose with Q-tips and baby oil. Lately Mom had been on Madison's case about pitching in more around the house, especially when it came to taking care of the dog.

The two went into the bathroom. Madison opened the medicine chest and grabbed the necessary supplies. Then she carried Phin downstairs to clean him up and take him for a walk.

When she got to the foot of the stairs, however, the doorbell rang. Phin let out a howl, jumped out of her arms, and raced to the door, ready to see who was waiting on the porch. Madison followed behind him. Through the peephole Madison spied Fiona, wearing a wide grin. She opened the door with a loud "Ta-da!"

But Fiona wasn't alone.

Although Madison didn't see them standing there at first, Fiona's twin brother, Chet; her sort-of boyfriend (who was also Madison's best guy friend), Walter "Egg" Diaz; Drew Maxwell; and Hart were also standing there. Everyone rubbed their hands together to beat away the outdoor chill.

4

Phin jumped up and down frantically when he saw the crowd of kids. Then he made a beeline for Chet's leg.

"Incoming!" Egg teased.

Drew snorted with laughter.

Chet backed up and nearly tumbled off the top porch step.

Phin barked again and the boys started to play with him, pretending to grab his tail and tossing him a chewed-up rubber ball that had been sitting on the porch.

"What are *you* doing here?" Madison asked.

"Egg brought his copy of Disaster Zone, the latest video game," Fiona declared. "He said you wouldn't mind if we came over to play it on your computer, since our monitor is busted."

"It's been broken for two weeks," Chet growled.

"So everyone was over at your place just now?" Madison asked.

Fiona nodded. "All the guys came over after school. I was trying to work on my journal project, but I couldn't get anything done."

"I was working on my journal, too," Madison said. "I'm stuck."

"Have you talked to Aim?" Fiona asked. She was referring to Aimee Gillespie, their other best friend.

"Aimee's at ballet class," Madison said. "Or maybe she's at her dad's store. I can't remember. I only know she left school right at the bell."

"Maddie, can we come inside, or what?" Egg asked as he scooped Phin into his arms. "Is your mom home? Can we use the downstairs computer in her office, or should we use your laptop?"

Madison shrugged and laughed. Sometimes, when he needed something, Egg acted as though he lived at her house. But Madison and Egg had been friends for forever, so she didn't mind. Neither did Mom.

"Well, well," Mom said, emerging from the kitchen with a look of surprise on her face when she saw everyone. "So the troops have arrived."

Hart and Drew, who hadn't said much up until that point, sheepishly said their polite hellos to Madison's mom. Everyone piled into the living room and took seats on every available couch and chair. Phin loved all the attention, especially when the kids played with the back of his neck, his favorite place to be scratched.

"Hi, Mrs. Finn," Fiona chirped, flipping her braids.

"Hello, Fiona, Chet, Drew, Hart, Egg . . ." Mom said. Even though Egg's name was Walter, Mom used the nickname. Fiona and Egg's parents were the only people who used his proper name.

Madison didn't know what to say. She clung to the corner of the couch, the only remaining seat. Hart was on her left.

"Gee, I've never been in your house before," Hart mumbled.

"Yeah, you have," Drew corrected his cousin. "Haven't you?"

Fiona raised her eyebrows and smiled at Madison with an all-knowing BFF look that said, *You WISH Hart had been in your house before. . . .*

Madison lifted one hand up to test the temperature of her cheek. Was she blushing? Any mention of her and Hart usually gave her a momentary fever.

"I don't think Hart's ever been here before," Madison said. "Except maybe on the front porch. I mean, we usually hang out at Aimee's or Fiona's or Drew's or somewhere else. Don't we?"

"Well, you have a nice house," Hart said, loud enough that Madison's mom could hear.

Mom smiled and bowed her head. "Thank you, Hart." She straightened a pile of magazines on the coffee table and picked up a few bags of videotapes packed in large yellow envelopes that were leaning up against one wall. She was in the middle of sending out a publicity mailing for Budge Films. Her offices were too busy to handle it that week, she explained, so she had decided to send out copies of her latest documentary to friends and partners in the business by herself. Madison had helped her figure out the postage and apply the labels earlier that weekend.

Egg picked up a small glass penguin from a side table. Madison leaped out of her seat to grab it from him.

"Careful! My mom got that in the antarctic," Madison said.

Mom looked out from behind an armful of stuffed envelopes and laughed. "Maddie, honey bear, I got that in Iceland. And that's a long way off from the south pole. . . ."

Everyone laughed—even Madison.

"Whoopsie," she said, giggling. "Guess I'm about ready to flunk my next geography test, right?"

"You and me both," Hart said, smiling.

Madison smiled right back, and from across the room Fiona raised her eyebrows again.

Mom got a bowl of chips from the kitchen and passed out bottles of root beer to everyone in the room except Chet, who said root beer made him sick to his stomach. As everyone dug into the snack, Egg, with a flourish, produced the Disaster Zone CD-ROM.

"This was the *last* copy at Video Palace in the mall," Egg announced. "*Mi mami* got it for me. She rocks."

Egg's mother, Senora Diaz, was always up on the latest trends and games. She also happened to be a Spanish teacher at Far Hills Junior High.

"Let's go into your mom's office," Egg said.

"Actually, I think my mom's working," Madison said softly. "We should leave her office alone. But we can go up to my room and play the game on my laptop."

"Thanks, Maddie. I think that's a good idea,"

Mom said, overhearing Maddie. "Why don't you bring the chips and drinks upstairs, too? But be careful. I just cleaned up there."

With Phin following behind, the group headed upstairs to Madison's room to play Disaster Zone. Upon opening her pink door, with the very large DO NOT DISTURB ME sign on it, Madison was relieved to see that she had, in fact, made her bed that morning. And fortunately there were no bras hanging on doorknobs or random articles of clothing lying on the windowsill. *That* would have been a real-life disaster zone, for sure.

Fiona, who had been in Madison's room dozens of times before, threw herself across Madison's bed without a second thought. The guys were a little awkward, especially Hart. He didn't seem to know where to sit or stand, so he just stuffed his hands in his pockets and looked around.

Chet made his way over to Madison's desk and searched her bulletin board for something he could make a joke about. He was always looking to make fun of something or someone. Drew and Egg wasted no time. They sat at Madison's desk chair, placed their root-beer bottles on the desk, and immediately booted up the game CD.

A screen flashed orange and red. An image of flames appeared and then quickly formed the words *Disaster Zone*. Everything flashed bright yellow, and in the background was the sound of loud sirens.

Then another screen popped up that read ARE YOU IN? CLICK HERE TO BEGIN GAME. Underneath the words was a single, flickering flame.

Hart went over behind the other guys as they clicked on the flame. The whole screen went white with a sizzling flash. The boys hooted.

Madison went over to the bed to sprawl out next to Fiona, but she stopped herself.

Oh, no! she thought, remembering her journaling page. Was it still on the computer screen? Had Egg deleted it? Had he *read* it? She quickly hopped off the bed and raced over to her desk, elbowing her way into the huddle of guys.

"Wait, wait," Madison said. "I have something . . . on the . . . computer. . . ." Madison pressed the ESCAPE key. The screen went blank.

"Huh? What happened?" Drew asked in a bewildered tone.

Egg's eyes opened wide. "Maddie!" he cried. He tried clicking a few keys, but the game would not restart. Madison couldn't find her document, either.

"You killed it," Chet said.

"I did not," Madison said. "I didn't kill anything."

"What was so important that you had to destroy the game?" Egg asked, lightly punching Madison in the arm. He was only half serious, but his punch kind of hurt.

"Hey, Egg, this is *my* laptop!" Madison said, punching him back, harder.

"Walter!" Fiona said, jumping off the bed. "Maddie was working on her journal."

"You mean that dorky assignment we got in school?" Chet asked.

"It is not dorky," Madison said. "What is wrong with keeping a journal?"

"I can't stand writing in a notebook. It's so . . . Middle Ages," Egg joked.

"So, what did you write about?" Drew asked Madison.

"I'm not telling you what I write in my journal!" Madison said.

"You're right," Egg said. "It's private."

Madison was shocked. Egg was rushing to her defense? He was usually the ringleader, the one who teased her mercilessly. Where was the crazy joke that he always delivered? His next words were even more shocking.

"Sorry, Maddie," Egg said. "I'll chill out."

As Madison picked her jaw up off the floor, she realized why Egg was acting contrite. *Fiona*. Duh.

Egg didn't want to look dumb or pushy in front of the girl he really liked.

Fiona responded accordingly, batting her eyelashes, or at least that's what Madison thought she saw. There was an awkward silence again.

"We should probably go," Hart said, slouching forward, his hands still in his pockets.

"No, no. Don't go," Madison said quickly. "I

mean, you don't have to go. I like having you here. Phin likes your being here, too. I mean, he likes *all* of you being here. . . . Why don't we go on bigfishbowl or something?"

"Oh!" Egg's face lit up. "Wait! Wait a minute! I know what we can do! Man, this is brilliant."

"You and your brilliant ideas," Chet moaned.

"What is it, Walter?" Fiona asked sweetly.

"Let me show you."

As Egg clicked away, Madison prayed that his fingers wouldn't slip and cause him to select one of her e-mail messages or open the secret folder on her desktop that held her files. She had visions of Hart standing there while a dozen different files carrying his name opened up.

    📁 Hart Jones
    📁 Hart (Continued)
    📁 Mr. & Mrs. Jones
    📁 The One
    📁 Him

Just like that, every detail about her crush would be on display for the world to see. And Hart would probably laugh so hard that his head would explode. This situation was getting a little too close for Maddie's comfort.

Thankfully, Egg bypassed all of Madison's private

documents and headed right for bigfishbowl's blog area. The screen went blue with tiny bubbles as the word BLOGGERFISHBOWL appeared on a giant fish swimming toward them. The fish looked 3-D, a lot like the "Ask the Blowfish" fish that swam around on the fortune-telling area of the site.

Phin rubbed up against Madison's leg. In the face of all of the distractions, he was demanding attention again. As Phinnie purred (because sometimes happy dogs purr, even louder than cats do), Madison read aloud the text that appeared on-screen.

Welcome to BLOGGERFISHBOWL!
Here are some answers to your most important questions.
What's BLOGGERFISHBOWL about?
This site is where you can get FREE, fun, online diary pages that you update through your Web browser. All you have to do is type. And if you know HTML, you can add funky design to your pages. Za-Zam!
How private is my diary?
You have the choice whether or not to list your diary in the member's area. Click on "Bloggerfishbowl Members" for more information. To be extra safe, all areas on the site have password protection. Share your password only with good friends—or else.

"Hey, good friends," Egg joked in a low voice.

"The password is Disaster Zone." He typed the words into the computer in the blank space where it said to enter a password. His fingers danced over the keyboard. Madison wished she could type as fast as he could.

Seconds later, the screen blinked: PASSWORD APPROVED. Everyone stared at the flashing cursor.

"Now what?" Chet asked.

"Wait," Egg said. "The home page will come up. It's my official blog for the Disaster Zone video game. Can't you see?"

Madison rolled her eyes. "Egg, it's a blank page."

"Good one, Egger!" Chet laughed out loud.

Drew snorted.

"Well, it's a work in progress," Egg said, sneering. As he closed the page with a loud grunt, Madison spotted an icon in the lower right-hand corner of her screen. Her missing journal page!

Before she could say anything, Egg clicked it.

Madison cringed. There was nothing she could do now.

"Gee, Maddie," Drew said with a grin. "Is this what you were so worried about us seeing?"

"It's a blank page, too!" Chet said, laughing again.

Madison glanced over at Fiona with a feeble smile and mouthed the word *phew*.

Chapter 2

Madison stuck her hand down into the bottom of her orange bag, but she couldn't find a pen. She was hoping to take a few minutes before the start of science class to finish her homework. It was a biology work sheet, and she was supposed to fill in definitions for words like *DNA*, *RNA*, and *genome*. Naturally, she'd spent most of the night before writing in her journal instead.

Mr. Danehy stood up at the front of class, coughing. His eyes watered, and his nose was running. He had a clump of tissue in his hand. No one wanted to approach him—or even talk to him, not even Ivy (who had proclaimed that she had a crush on him once—Go figure!).

Nope. Mr. Danehy was grouchy enough on a *good* day. No one would risk his wrath on a day when he was *sick*.

With only moments before the second bell rang, Ivy squeezed herself onto her stool next to Madison at the lab table.

"Did you finish the homework?" Ivy asked. She snapped her mint gum, even though gum was against the rules in the classroom.

Madison didn't answer. She knew that would irritate Ivy. And it did.

"Did you hear me?" Ivy said in a huff. "I asked you if—"

"I heard you," Madison said. She didn't need chewing gum to snap back at Ivy. "And I haven't finished the homework, but even if I had, I wouldn't share it with you."

"You don't have to be so nasty," Ivy growled.

She muttered something else; Madison was pretty sure she had said, "You must have wicked PMS," but Madison didn't know how to respond, since she hadn't actually gotten her period yet. Was it physically possible to have PMS before having started to get your period? And why was Madison the only girl in the seventh grade who hadn't gotten hers?

Ivy flipped her red hair. It smelled like hair spray and some kind of perfume that made Madison's nose itch.

"Fine," Ivy said, snapping her gum again. "Be

that way." She reached into her own leather bag and pulled out a composition notebook.

Madison eyed the notebook carefully. It was Ivy's journal for the class assignment. On the cover Ivy had applied a sticker that read: "Princess." Madison knew she shouldn't look, but she couldn't help herself. She squinted to read the inscription next to the sticker.

Ivy turned the page.

Mr. Danehy crossed his arms, cleared his throat, and gazed at the class with watery eyes. He seemed to be sweating, too.

"Can we please put away our personal items? I have something important—" Mr. Danehy tried to finish his sentence but started coughing again and rushed out the door of the classroom. As the second bell rang, Mr. Danehy's loud, hacking cough echoed up and down the corridor. Kids snickered. Madison was convinced that students in the next building could hear.

The whole time, Ivy kept writing in her journal as if she didn't see or hear any of the commotion. Madison was tempted to glance at Ivy's page again, but she resisted. She turned her head.

From across the room, Hart caught her eye. He had been talking to another kid at his lab table, but he smiled when he saw Madison look at him. She had never noticed how crooked Hart's teeth were on top. How could she have never seen that? she wondered. She was seeing a lot of things from this angle, like the word "Sk8r" on his sneakers. She knew that that was Hart's screen name.

Hart smiled again.

"Dis-as-ter zone," Madison mouthed, tipping her head as if to indicate Ivy—and Egg's video game, of course.

"What did you just say?" Ivy asked, looking up. She flipped her hair again.

Madison tried not to smirk. "Um . . . nothing."

"Oh. *Right*," Ivy said. She glanced over in Hart's direction and then back at Madison again. It was always the same between Madison and Ivy—like a competition that had been launched the moment junior high school began. Who would get Hart? Who would Hart like better?

Madison was pretty sure that she'd won the first leg of the race to get Hart's heart. Everyone, including Egg, Fiona, Aimee, and Drew (who was Hart's cousin, so he *really* knew the deal), said that the crush feeling was mutual between Hart and Madison. Then there was the almost date. Madison and Hart had *almost* gone to the movies as a couple. Ivy hadn't had any of those experiences. She and Hart never went to any movies—or anywhere— together except maybe the school lunchroom, and that didn't count.

While Ivy simmered and tried to make Hart look at her (and not at Madison), Madison glanced down at her journal again. It lay open, uncovered, on the lab table. Her brain said, *"Look away! Look away!"* But it was as if Madison's eyes were magnets drawn to a magnetic field.

Madison read the words *My life is just so . . .*

Ivy's hand was partly covering the page.

Just so *what*?

At that moment, Mr. Danehy came back into the classroom, his hands still over his mouth. His face looked blotchy, as if he'd been coughing a lot. And of course, he had. He looked sweatier than ever. Although Madison wasn't a huge fan of her science teacher, she was a teeny bit worried.

"Class, I need to walk down the hall for a moment. Would you please open your books to chapter six? I want you to memorize all the terms on page ninety-one. I'll have the hall monitor come in and watch the class while I'm gone."

Madison was relieved. Now he wouldn't be collecting the homework right away—and maybe not even until tomorrow. It gave her a chance to finish, and to spy on more of what Ivy had written.

But the moment Madison glanced over again, that voice inside her head screamed, *"Stop looking at Ivy's journal!"* She put her head down on the table with a thud.

Ouch. Madison's head throbbed. She hadn't meant to bonk it.

"You okay, Maddie?" Ivy asked, her voice

feigning niceness as if she were the wolf in *Little Red Riding Hood*. "Look. You don't have to hit your head just because Mr. Danehy's leaving. I mean, I know you like him and all that. . . ."

Ivy laughed, but Madison heard it as more of a witch's cackle. Ivy was like the wolf *and* the witch rolled into one.

"You look a little pale, Maddie," Ivy continued. "Hey, you're not going to throw up or something, are you? Because I just can't deal with barf."

Madison lifted her chin off the table and peered into Ivy's green eyes. "You can't deal with anything," Madison said softly.

"Right. Whatever." Ivy clucked her tongue. "I wish I didn't have you for a lab partner. I mean, it's not even worth copying your homework. It's not like you get all A's."

Madison tried hard not to snarl when Ivy said that. She turned to say something clever. But what she saw was the journal. And this time, Ivy's hand wasn't blocking the words.

My life is just so . . . perfect.

Just so perfect. *That* was what Ivy had written? *Perfect?*

Now Madison really did feel like throwing up. She felt bad that she'd looked at the page to begin with. Sneaking a peek was the wrong thing to do, and she knew it. But Madison now felt sick because of *what* Ivy had written, too.

What was it about Miss Poison Ivy's life that was so perfect?

Ivy grabbed her journal and moved next to her drone friend Rose, leaving Madison alone at the corner of the lab table.

It was a good thing. Without the distraction, Madison managed to finish her homework questions and read the assigned chapter. Thankfully, Mr. Danehy never returned. If he had, there surely would have been a surprise pop quiz or something equally painful.

At the final bell, the monitor dismissed everyone. Madison moved to the front of class.

Was she imagining things . . . or had Hart hustled over to be next to her as they exited the room? The only thing better would have been if he'd elbowed Ivy into the wall on his way over.

"Did you finish all the work?" Hart asked.

"Yeah," Madison admitted with a sheepish grin. "You?"

"Yeah," Hart said. "Looked like Ivy and you were arguing."

"Big surprise," Madison said with a sigh.

"She gets weirder every day," Hart said, nodding.

"I actually thought you liked her," Madison said.

"Me? Like Ivy? Uh . . . not exactly," Hart said. "She's pretty and all that, but sometimes she's just . . . well, I said it. She's a big weirdo."

"She likes *you*," Madison said.

"Whatever," Hart mumbled.

Madison didn't know what to say next. She considered saying, "Hart, don't you know I like you? I want to date you. I'm your dream girl."

But she said nothing.

They walked past a few banks of lockers in silence. When they finally reached the staircase, Hart needed to go up, and Madison needed to go down.

"Later, Finnster," Hart said. "Er . . . Maddie. Sorry, I guess I should stop calling you Finnster. I know it bugs you."

"Yeah, well . . ." Madison stopped herself in midsentence. "No, Finnster isn't so bad. I like it. Don't stop. Really."

"Really?"

Madison nodded. "I just need to think of a good nickname for you."

"Uh . . . Egg calls me Loser sometimes," Hart joked. "Or Weasel."

"I was thinking more like Hunk," Madison said.

"Huh?" Hart blinked. "What did you just say?"

"What?" Madison's face froze. She wanted to run. Her stomach was like a trampoline inside—*bounce, bounce, bounce.* Her knees started to quake. She couldn't take it back. Had she really just called him Hunk? Oh. My. God.

"I said, 'Dork,'" Madison replied quickly. "Why? What did you think I said?"

"Oh, yeah, that's me. *Super* Dork, actually," Hart said with a goofy wink.

Madison's entire body was on the verge of collapse—she was *that* embarrassed. She slung her bag across her back and adjusted the shoulders of her pink-flecked sweater so that it wasn't all bunched up at the shoulders.

"Gee," she said a moment later, pushing through the doors to the staircase, "gotta dash. Bye!" She raced down toward the bottom floor.

Hart barely had time to yell out, "See you later!" before Madison was gone.

Once she was out of sight, Madison searched for a bathroom stall where she could could lock herself in and recover. Or maybe she could stuff her head inside a locker and scream? Conversations with Hart were an endless series of missteps. Either he seemed interested in her and she seemed uninterested in him, or vice versa. Either they had nothing at all to say, or they would start talking and Madison would say all the wrong things. Why couldn't her life turn out more like a TV movie of the week? Madison was ready for the boy, the sunset, and the big embrace. She just needed to work on her lines.

After school, Aimee met Madison so that they could walk home together. Madison didn't mention the Hart/Hunk thing. She was still too embarrassed to tell anyone.

Aimee seemed down in the dumps. Madison asked what was wrong, but Aimee wasn't talking much, and she just grunted in reply. Madison started rambling, to fill in the silence between them.

"How was ballet yesterday?" Madison asked. No reply. "So, you missed a funny time at my house. Egg and Drew and Fiona and Chet and everyone came over. Egg was showing us some new video game called Disaster Zone. And he made this blog page devoted to it. I didn't realize there's this whole Bloggerfishbowl section on bigfishbowl.com now. Did you?"

Aimee shrugged. "I'm tired. Do we have to talk?"

Madison stopped in her tracks. "Since when do you want to stop talking?"

"Since today," Aimee said. "My ballet teacher . . ." She stopped walking, too. And then she dissolved into tears.

"What's wrong?" Madison cried, hugging her friend.

"My classes were canceled for a week. My teacher is sick, Maddie. Real sick."

"I'm sorry," Madison said. It was the only thing she could think of to say.

"She didn't want us to know about it, but then she sat us all down after class yesterday and told us the real deal. We were all crying. I've felt like crying all day. She has breast cancer. That's so serious, right? She's the best teacher in the whole world, Maddie."

"Wow," Madison said. She'd only known one other person who had had breast cancer before that moment. It was a friend of her mom's from work.

The year before, her mom and the friend had walked in a Race for the Cure event together. Madison had tagged along.

The girls said their good-byes in front of Madison's house, and Aimee walked on to her house, a few doors down. Madison climbed up her porch, exhausted by the long day at school and all of the emotional things that had happened since the late-afternoon bell. She tore off her jacket and sweater and kicked off her sneakers. Phin was right there with a few welcome-home doggy snorts. He licked her foot, too.

"Good dog," Madison said as she gave him some kisses on the top of his furry head.

Mom was pacing up and down in the kitchen, talking to herself. Classical music was playing on the radio. She had her hair swept up in a ponytail and was wearing a plum-colored crepe dress and black heels.

"Hello, honey bear," Mom said, blowing Madison a kiss.

"Why are you so dressed up?" Madison asked.

"Oh, no reason," Mom said. "I had an afternoon meeting today, that's all."

"Really?" Madison said, climbing into a kitchen chair. She tossed her bag on the table and pulled out her laptop. It was almost out of power, so she plugged it in to charge it.

"How was your day?" Mom asked.

"Fine," Madison said. "Aimee just told me sad news, though."

"What?" Mom asked.

"Her dance teacher is sick. She has to stop teaching for a while. She has breast cancer," Madison explained.

"Oh," Mom said. Her face fell, and she looked away.

"What's wrong, Mom?"

Mom cleared her throat and smoothed the counter with her hand. "Oh, nothing. I was just thinking of Grandma Finn."

Madison's grandmother, on her father's side, had died before Madison was born.

"She had breast cancer, too, you know," Mom said.

"She *did*?" Madison wondered how she could have missed hearing that important fact.

"It just seems like so many women I know have it these days," Mom said, sounding very sad.

"Really?" Madison asked. "I remember your friend from work. Who else?"

"Oh," Mom said, staring into space. "No one. No one in particular, honey bear. Should we order a pizza for dinner tonight?"

Madison's stomach rumbled at the thought of pepperoni. She got off the chair and pulled the Pizza Pie menu out of a drawer.

From across the kitchen, Phin howled.

Madison smiled. He'd want a piece all for himself—minus the pepperoni, of course.

Chapter 3

For a Monday night, Madison was up very late. It was the pizza, she figured. Two and a half slices had given her a whopper of a bellyache. That was twice as much food as Madison usually ate for dinner. All the same, it didn't stop her from chewing a stick of gum that she had found inside her desk drawer.

Madison's computer beeped. She had an e-mail. She tapped the keyboard to retrieve it, but saw that the message was only spam. The uninvited e-mail was addressed to a Mr. M. Finn and advertised a miracle drug to make hair grow. Madison quickly hit DELETE and surfed over to bigfishbowl.com.

At the site menu, there was an option to surf to the pages most recently visited. Madison wanted to check out Egg's Disaster Zone page again. At school that day, he had claimed that he would be working on it all night, so Madison was curious to see what he had added. Did it look any less like a blank page?

Madison couldn't access the first page link she hit. She went to the Bloggerfishbowl main menu to find the SEARCH function. It asked her to enter a word, so Madison typed the word *disaster*. A list popped up, and she scrolled through. People had chosen funny names for their blogs.

```
Disaster Area
Disaster Land: My Life
Disaster Sister!!!
Disaster Zone
Dis Me L8r, Homeboy
Don't Ask: The Whole Truth
Don't Forget Me
Don't Worry Page
```

Madison clicked on Egg's page, but apparently he hadn't done any work yet. It was still as blank as before. She hit the BACK browser and looked over the list again. What else was on some of those blogs? She double-clicked on *Disaster Land: My Life*. A blue page popped up. In the background, the blogger had inserted images of raindrops. Each text entry was a poem—a lame poem as far as Madison could tell, although she knew it wasn't fair to call people's ideas or work lame when she didn't know them personally.

She hit the BACK browser once again and selected another page. *Dis Me L8r, Homeboy* seemed like a funny one. But when she clicked on it, the page listed underneath opened up instead.

Madison started reading. But she didn't get very far.

```
Don't Ask: The Whole Truth
A blog by Vicki (aka Bigwheels)
```

Bigwheels?
Madison's eyes bugged out. She nearly fell out of her chair and choked on her bubble gum. But she kept reading.

```
    I know I need to just relax but how can
I relax when I don't get any sleep either?
I think I'm going to check out one of the
chat rooms Dad told me about. I never knew
it affected so many kids. I also found out
that I can volunteer down @ the speech
center in Seattle. I don't think I'll be
working with kids who have autism but I
will probably learn a lot.
    --BW
```

Madison took a deep breath and reread the blog entry on her screen. This was no coincidence. This had to be BW, aka Vicki, aka Bigwheels, her keypal. There couldn't be two Bigwheelses in the world, could there? Madison's mind raced with questions. She clicked another key, marked PROFILE.

Screen Name: Bigwheels
Home Sweet Home: USA
Favorite Place: My basement, because
that's where my computer is now!
Favorite Person: My brother Eddie and my
sister Mel and my keypal 2 b/c she's nicer
than nice

Madison stopped reading. There was no doubt now.

This was her Bigwheels.

How could Madison's keypal have kept a blog on bigfishbowl.com, the place where they had first connected? And how could she have kept it a secret? It was too much to think about. Madison pressed the ON/OFF button on her laptop without even logging off.

Phin hopped up onto Madison's bed with a rope chew toy in his mouth. It was frayed and wet at the ends, but Madison started up a game of tug-of-war to take her mind off the blog. Every time Phinnie pulled the rope one way, Madison pulled harder in the opposite direction. Halfway through the game, she yanked the toy right out of Phin's little mouth. He yelped.

Madison sat there on the carpet, a little stunned. She'd pulled too hard. But she knew why. She was angry—really angry. She felt betrayed by Bigwheels. She'd been certain that she and her keypal shared *all* of the important stuff. They talked about boys they liked, teachers they didn't like, and everything annoying that their parents did. Bigwheels always had funny stories to tell about her family. Madison loved hearing what life was like with a brother and a sister, since she had neither. But she had never heard anything about this blog—or the information it gave.

Why hadn't she told Madison she was volunteering somewhere? After all, Madison always told her about her own experiences volunteering at the Far Hills Animal Clinic.

Phin yelped again. His ears went back, and his little curlicue tail went down. Now he was upset, too.

"I'm so sorry, Phinnie," Madison said softly, leaning over. She rolled over, pulled him onto her tummy, and gave him a kiss. He cheered up right away and trotted back to get his chew toy.

Madison got up off the floor to power up her computer again. She was obsessed with what she'd seen on bigfishbowl.com. She needed to know why Bigwheels had not told her about the blog—and she needed to know now.

"Maddie, are you busy?" Mom yelled from downstairs.

Madison yelled back immediately: "Yes!"

"Well, I need you. Just for a moment. Can you help me?"

Phin scampered out of the room when he heard Mom's voice.

Can you help me? It was Mom's typical refrain. Madison had often joked that her middle name should have been Help. Since the Big D, Mom often relied on Madison for assistance with things around the house, even though the reality was that Madison wasn't much good at helping. She couldn't locate a wall stud on which to hang a picture or find a washer in a toolbox filled with screws. But Mom asked for help anyhow. And Madison obliged. She liked being helpful—usually. Right now, though, she didn't want to move from this spot. She needed to get back to the blog.

"Maddie?" Mom appeared at Madison's bedroom door. "Just for a minute, honey bear. Okay? I know you're doing homework."

Madison hit the STANDBY button on her computer. She didn't want Mom to see that she wasn't doing the homework she'd promised to do before bedtime. A Bengal tiger screen saver appeared in the nick of time.

As usual, Mom was still working. Madison thought it was cool to have a mom who made movies—well, documentaries. But sometimes it was a drag that Mom worked so much, especially late at night. Madison wished her mom would take time off. It had been a long time since she and Mom had spent an entire day hanging out, just the two of them.

"We need to move these cartons. . . ." Mom

explained. "The boxes are too heavy to move by myself."

Madison was glad that the job took only a few minutes. By the time she climbed back upstairs, her e-mailbox was blinking with two new messages.

The first was from Dad.

From: JeffFinn
To: MadFinn
Subject: Dinner Times Two for Four?
Date: Mon 11 Oct 8:49 PM

Hey, honey—I want to do dinner twice
this week if that's ok. Tomorrow
it's just you and me. Let's go to
French Toast, just the two of us? I
know you liked their crispy-chicken
basket. Then, Stephanie and I want
you to come over again this Sunday.
Stephanie's making something special
for dinner. You can even bring
Phinnie if you like. That makes four
of us. It's up to you.

BTW: here is a joke that made me
think of you!

How does a smart kid spend hours on
her homework every night when she
sleeps for 12 hours? She puts the
homework under her mattress!

Let me know when we should pick
you up Sunday. I think your mom
may have other plans, so we'll coor-
dinate.

Love,

Dad

P.S.: We're thinking about getting a
pet. Got any leads from the animal
shelter in town?

Maddie clicked REPLY and sent Dad a note saying
that she was looking forward to dinner. She didn't
go into too much detail, however. She was way too
eager to get to the next e-mail in her mailbox and
then get in touch with Bigwheels.

```
FROM                    SUBJECT
☒ Sk8ingboy      DZ
```

Madison gulped. The second e-mail was from Hart.
Her eyes skimmed over the header and went right to
the body of the message.

```
From: Sk8ingboy
To: TheEggMan, Wetwins, W_Wonka7,
MadFinn
Subject: DZ
Date: Mon 11 Oct 9:12 PM
```
Hey, guys, my dad just called the

FH rink and the dude there said we
can play next wkend which is cool
so let's find other guys and we'll
be hooked up. I was thinking maybe
we could go over to Drew's to play
the Zone again b4 we sk8 since the
game @ Maddie's was so lame. OK.
E-me 18r.

HJ

The game at Maddie's was so lame.
Madison squinted to make sure she had read that correctly. Lame? She felt the hairs standing up on the back of her neck. As far as she was concerned, as of that very moment, Hart was the lame one.

Madison scanned the names at the top of the e-mail. He obviously had sent the note to Madison by mistake. She couldn't exactly be mad at him for that. But as usual, the doubts started to creep in. She'd come upstairs after dinner and logged on to her laptop as she did every other night, expecting to surf around casually and check out the blogs and her e-mail. But now Madison was utterly thrown. Bigwheels didn't want to share. Hart thought she was lame.

Was this how people really felt? Why couldn't they tell her the truth? Why couldn't everyone just keep it real?

Instead of opening up a new file, Madison

reached for her FHJH composition notebook. She was inspired to write something by hand—and it fit in perfectly with the second topic Mr. Gibbons had doled out in class that day.

Journaling #2
Topic: Everyone has a good scar story. Tell all the details about how you got your best scar.

At first, Madison was thinking she would write about the long scar she had on her left ankle. She had gotten it when she was eight, when her foot had gotten wedged in the chains on her bike and she had yanked her leg out too fast. Even after it had started to heal, the scab kept pulling off whenever she rode her bike—which was every day. As a result, it had left a spaghetti-thin scar around the circumference of Madison's ankle.

Although that was a fun scar story, Madison now knew the ankle scar wasn't the scar she would write about.

She picked up her purple pencil. Even though the end was gnawed, it still worked fine for writing.

My Scar
It's hard to admit this to anyone except my dog, but my best scar (really the worst) comes from when my parents got divorced. It seems like

since the Big D, it got harder to know what I could trust. I'm not totally insecure (only sometimes), but this year in seventh grade I wonder all the time who really likes me and who is telling me the real deal. Do people sometimes make up stuff just to be nice? I guess I even do that sometimes. But whenever it happens (like now) I feel like someone is ripping off a big scab and what's left is my scar. Does that make any sense or am I

Madison stopped writing. She quickly tore out the page, crumpled it up, and threw it into the orange plastic wastebasket. Without missing a beat, she turned to the next blank page, rewrote the heading, and wrote a new paragraph describing her ankle scar after all.

Ten minutes later she brushed her teeth and crawled into bed.

It was hard to fall asleep. Madison's mind buzzed with thoughts of Hart gossiping about her (and how lame she was) with the other guys, and of Bigwheels writing in her blog that she hadn't told Madison about. Just what was autism, anyway? Madison would have to do a dictionary search online. Then she would write an e-mail directly to Bigweels and ask her what was going on.

Of course, eventually all of those thoughts faded away, or at least morphed into images of the jumping sheep that Madison counted until she fell fast asleep. After a while, Phin was sleeping, too. His little paws danced as if he were running in his doggy dreams.

When Mom finished her work, some time after midnight, she tucked them both into bed and closed Madison's laptop. Although Madison was asleep and didn't hear it, Mom whispered something very real into Madison's ear.

"Good night, honey bear. Thank you for being such a beautiful daughter. You are my moon and stars, and I love you more than anything—no matter what."

With that, Mom turned out the light and called it a night.

Phinnie started snoring.

Aimee was in better spirits by Tuesday morning.

So was Madison. All of the distressing thoughts of the night before had faded after a good night's sleep.

Aimee met Madison out in front of her house on Blueberry Street. She walked over with Mrs. Gillespie and Blossom, their basset hound. The moment that Blossom turned in to the Finn walk, with her snout to the ground, she must have smelled Phinnie, because she charged up the porch steps panting. The two dogs were best friends, just like their owners. They sniffed and chased each other's tail, as happy dogs do.

"Morning, Francine," Mrs. Gillespie called out to Madison's mom. "I took you up on your offer. It's been too long!"

Mom invited Mrs. Gillespie in for a cup of morning coffee. Madison and Aimee enjoyed watching their mothers sit down together to talk. It happened rarely, but it gave the girls a glimpse into what their own friendship might be in twenty or thirty years. Aimee joked that if they never found the perfect guys, at least they had each other. Fiona Waters and Lindsay Frost, their other good friends, were in on that promise, too. The four vowed to be sitting together in rocking chairs, still talking about the enemy, boys, and bigfishbowl.com when they were much older.

As Mom and Mrs. Gillespie walked inside, they whispered as if they were sharing some kind of secret. For a brief moment, Madison wondered what the fuss was about. But she didn't dwell on it. She grabbed her orange bag and then grabbed Aimee's wrist.

The girls danced back down the path and onto the street as they headed for school, waving goodbye to their mothers and the two dogs.

"Rowowoworooooo!" Phin howled. Blossom howled, too.

"So," Aimee declared, skipping in front of Madison. Aimee could never just walk like a normal person. She skipped, floated, spun—everything a dancer would do onstage. "I heard something that will just make you insane!"

"Oh, no," Madison sighed. "I'm not so sure I want to hear this."

"I got this information from my brother Doug," Aimee said. He was the youngest of her three brothers. The others were Billy, a college student, and Dean, a high-school senior. Aimee went to them for advice and sometimes even gossip. This time it had been for gossip.

"Doug only cares about baseball," Madison joked.

"Yeah, well, it's the off-season," Aimee joked back. "And he swears that he has good sources. Don't you wanna hear it?"

Madison shrugged. "I guess."

"Okay. Prepare yourself!" Aimee gestured wildly. "Ivy Daly is dating a high-school sophomore. High school!"

"What?" Madison's eyes popped open wide. It was common knowledge that another one of their junior-high-school classmates, Monica Jennings, dated older guys. But Ivy? Madison couldn't believe it. Was *that* why Ivy had written in her class journal that life was so perfect?

"Who is it?" Madison asked.

"I don't have a name," Aimee said. "Doug says he goes to Dunn Manor High. The guys know him from pickup football games or something. He was bragging that Ivy is really hot."

Dunn Manor Junior High was the rival school to Far Hills Junior High. Usually Madison saw guys from Dunn when her school played soccer or hockey games with the other school. The guys who went

41

there always seemed cuter than the guys at her school. Gramma Helen would have said that that meant that Madison and her friends had a case of "the grass is greener on the other side of the fence." They always wanted whatever it was that they couldn't have. Cute guys were their greener grass.

Of course, Madison didn't know any of the Dunn guys personally. She wouldn't have had a clue as to who Ivy's guy was even if Aimee had mentioned a name.

As they walked toward school, the brisk air whipped around Madison's neck and ears. She pulled her sweater tighter, wondering why she had not worn a warmer jacket. But, of course, her denim jacket with the cool embroidered lining was in the wash, and her other favorite, a brown coat, had a splatter of Freeze Palace's chocolate-cow milk shake on the front. Mom still hadn't taken that one over to the dry cleaner.

Aimee had clearly accepted the news of her dance teacher's illness by now. She was definitely back to her old self again. Translation: she wouldn't shut up. After a while, Madison stopped listening.

Aimee noticed.

"Maddie? Maddie! Are you ignoring me?" Aimee said very loudly, waving her arms in front of Madison's face.

"Huh? No way," Madison replied. "I totally heard every word you said. . . ."

"Get real," Aimee said. "You were spacing out on me. Thanks a lot. I have vital information about our classmates and you're spacing? That's great!"

"Vital information?" Madison asked. She giggled. "Nothing about Ivy is vital except the fact that she is terminally evil."

"And don't forget, fashion-challenged," Aimee added.

They both cracked up.

They met Fiona and Lindsay at the lockers before heading off to their English classes. Madison couldn't wait to hear what Mr. Gibbons had to say. She was eager to review the last journaling assignment and to get the new one. Fiona joined her on the way to Mr. Gibbons's classroom, and Aimee and Lindsay trotted off toward Mrs. Quill's classroom.

"Good morning, students," Mr. Gibbons said when all the members of the class had taken their seats and settled down.

Madison sat back in her chair, a smile on her face. She was loving school these days, especially this class. Was it possible for one class to make everything right with the world? After yesterday's surprise downers, she hoped so. She needed the cheering up.

"Let's start with . . . Lance," Mr. Gibbons said, pointing to one of Madison's classmates, an annoying guy (as far as Madison was concerned) who, along with Egg and Drew, was on the computer team that was responsible for inputting information and updates for the school Web site. Lance cleared his throat and began to read aloud from one of his journal entries.

When he started, Madison expected to laugh. She expected everyone to start laughing. But what he read wasn't funny at all. No one laughed. No one breathed.

"My scar story," Lance read, clearing his throat again, "is gross and weird, at least I think so. When I was a baby, like, way before I was even born, I had special surgery."

The class let out a collective "Ooooh!"

"Like, I had this problem with my heart," Lance continued. He bent his head as he read directly from his composition notebook.

Madison listened intently. She played with the edges of her own journal pages, ruffling them with her fingertips. Was this really Lance talking?

"That is very personal," Mr. Gibbons said, when Lance had finished reading. "Very impressive detail."

Madison nodded silently. She was impressed, too. Not only because Lance had read aloud from his journal (something she wasn't sure she was ready to do), but because what he had to say was so . . . real.

Long ago, at the start of school, Mr. Gibbons had told his class that there was only one thing they could be sure of in his seventh-grade section. He said that his students should expect the unexpected.

Madison couldn't believe how true that was.

After class, Fiona had to run off to the nurse's office to get an aspirin because she had a headache. Madison ducked into the bathroom and hooked her orange bag on the door of the stall.

While she was in there, a group of girls came in, whispering. One of them was crying.

Madison gasped.

It was Poison Ivy.

Madison listened intently, trying hard not to make noise. She tried peeking through the side of the door, but she couldn't really see.

It sounded as though Rose Thorn and Phony Joanie, Ivy's two drone friends, were trying to comfort her. Madison listened closely.

"I just don't think I can deal," Ivy announced dramatically.

"Yes, you can," Rose said. "You are so strong, Ivy. Everyone knows how strong you are."

Ivy hiccuped. She was crying again. Madison hadn't heard her cry like that since they were younger.

"I can't . . ." Ivy sniffled. "I can't believe I'm getting like this at school. . . ."

Joanie leaned down. She was peeking under the stalls! Madison lifted her feet up so they wouldn't see her. Then she put a hand over her mouth.

"Don't worry," Joanie announced. "No one's here."

Rose turned on the faucet. "Here, take this. Wipe your face."

"I can't . . ." Ivy sobbed. "I'll ruin my makeup."

Madison rolled her eyes. Her makeup? Of course, even when she was upset, Ivy wanted to look good. And what kind of problem was she crying about, anyway? Madison guessed it was the Dunn Manor guy. It had to be. That would be just the kind of problem that would make Ivy break down in the bathroom at school. Guy stuff.

Madison clenched her fists together and held her legs up higher, just in case someone peeked under the stalls again. She couldn't risk getting caught and branded a spy.

Ivy sniffled a little bit more. Madison had to strain to hear what she and her friends were saying now. She heard a few whispers, but couldn't make out the exact words.

". . . Be okay . . ." Joanie mumbled.

". . . Just keep it together. . . ." Rose said.

"Yeah, I know," Ivy said, her voice regaining its strength.

Madison took another deep breath and filled her cheeks with air. She heard Ivy, Rose, and Joanie pick up their stuff and walk out of the bathroom.

No talking, no sighing, no breathing. Not until they were gone.

The door squeaked and clicked.

Madison dropped her legs and opened the stall.

"*Maddie?*"

Madison froze. Ivy was still there, standing at the sink, wiping her nose. The drones had gone, but she had stayed behind, silent.

The two enemies stared each other down in the mirror.

"Were you in there the whole time?" Ivy asked, wiping her nose (and tears) some more.

"It's a free country," Madison said.

Ivy cocked her head to the side. "Um . . . what did you hear?"

"Nothing," Madison said.

Madison glanced over at Ivy's bag on the ledge by the windows. She could see Ivy's black-and-white journal poking up between the zippered sides. As soon as she saw Madison looking, Ivy grabbed the bag and pulled it close to her. The journal fell back inside.

"You'd better not have heard anything, Madison Finn," Ivy said menacingly. "And you'd better keep your big trap shut!"

Ivy wasn't crying anymore. She was yelling. She pushed the door hard and exited the bathroom.

Madison's knees felt a little wobbly. The whole incident had made her uncomfortable. *Had* she been spying?

As she went back over to the sink to wash her hands, Lindsay walked in.

"Hey, Maddie, I just saw Ivy leaving. Boy, did she

look upset," Lindsay said. "She's got such a major attitude. You know what I mean?"

"I know," Madison said. "What else is new?"

After school, Madison hustled toward home. Dad would be picking her up, and Madison needed to change out of her school clothes and put on something a little dressier for dinner.

As usual, Dad was late, but only by a few minutes. They sped over to French Toast, their hangout for Tuesday-night dinners. The maître d' served them an appetizer tray of pecan bread, crackers, herb-butter, cheddar sticks, and more. French Toast was one of those restaurants where some of the best stuff you got was what they served for free *before* the main course.

Madison and Dad talked their way through the meal. Even though Dad had remarried, he would still talk about the times with Mom and their days together as a family. Madison played along. Talking about the past meant that she didn't have to tell Dad what was *really* going on in her life.

She didn't mention Bigwheels's secret blog.

She avoided all discussion of Ivy's "perfect" life.

And she definitely didn't talk about Mom's unusually dressed-up outfits these days, whatever they meant. (Madison was beginning to think they meant something very interesting indeed, but she didn't want to admit it to herself—let alone to Dad.)

It was way more tiring not to say certain words or thoughts at dinner than to admit everything right then and there, out in the open. By the time the meal was over, keeping so many topics of discussion out of the conversation had left Madison exhausted. When Dad suggested they share a slice of flourless chocolate cake (usually the best part of the whole evening), Madison just shook her head.

"Let's go home now," Madison said.

"Maddie doesn't want dessert? Call the papers! What's wrong with you?"

"I don't know," Madison said. "Nothing. Every-thing. Nothing."

Dad didn't make Madison explain any more than that. He paid the check and gave Madison a warm hug, which was way more comforting than words. Then he drove her home.

As he often did, Dad walked Madison to the door. Mom answered the bell.

"Hello, Frannie," Dad said as he squeezed Madison's shoulder. "Don't you look nice tonight!"

Madison nodded. "Yeah, Mom. Where's the party?"

Mom's usual attire of sweatpants and a long shirt had been replaced by a long black dress with a turquoise-and-silver belt. On her feet she wore a pol-ished pair of new black boots.

"Thanks for taking Maddie tonight, Jeff," Mom said.

"You had a good night?" Dad asked Mom.

Did he know something? Madison wondered.

Mom grinned. "Splendid."

"Well, I'm off," Dad said with a clap of his hands and a kiss on Madison's forehead. He leaned over to give Phinnie a smooch, too.

Before he walked out the door, Dad smiled and patted Mom on the arm, and for a split second, Madison imagined that he was flirting with Mom and she with him again, which meant that maybe, just maybe, they still liked each other a little, which meant that there was a brief, teeny-weeny flicker of reconciliation in the air.

Of course, there wasn't. It was all a dream, but dreams like that always popped up, even now—a year after the Big D. Even now that Dad had married Stephanie.

Mom locked the door behind Dad and kissed Madison again.

"Gee, Mom, you look so pretty tonight," Madison said as she tugged off her jacket and shoes.

"Mmmm," Mom mumbled. "Thanks. You look pretty, too, Maddie. Did you and your father have a good meal?"

"Yeah. Sure," Madison said. "Did you go somewhere for dinner?"

"Oh, I ate a little," Mom said, burying her nose in a book.

"Big date, huh?" Madison joked.

Mom didn't answer right away. "I went for a drink with a friend," she said after a moment. "Nothing special."

"Oh," Madison said. "But didn't you go and get your hair done at Salon Pink yesterday?"

Mom looked back down at the book. "Yes," she said softly. "I did."

"How long was Mrs. Gillespie here this morning?" Madison asked.

"Aren't you just full of questions tonight? Let's see. . . . Aimee's mom was here for just about an hour. We had a nice, long chat. I've been working so hard lately. I miss dishing the dirt with my girlfriends."

"Dishing dirt?"

"Oh, you know. It's just a figure of speech, Maddie. Sharing all the gossip."

"Like, what gossip?" Madison asked.

Mom clucked her tongue. "There are some secrets that aren't meant to be shared."

"You're no fun. I'm going to bed," Madison said.

"Mmmm," Mom sighed again. "Give me a kiss first."

Madison leaned in for a kiss and a hug before heading upstairs. When she stepped into her bedroom, she saw Phin sleeping on top of her many pillows. He stirred a little, waiting for a pat on the head, but then went back to sleep.

Madison's laptop was still open on her desk, the

power still on from earlier that afternoon. She sat right down in front of it.

Mom had said that some secrets were not meant to be shared. That got Madison thinking. Was that how Bigwheels felt? Was that why she had kept the news of the blog from Madison?

Madison hit NEW.

```
From: MadFinn
To: Bigwheels
Subject: Bigfishbowl
Date: Tues 12 Oct 8:46 PM
Whassup? LTNE!

Well, things in my life are the
same. I need a new wardrobe, a new
haircut, ha-ha. Actually, my stepmom
gave me some hand-me-down sweaters
that fit me and they are retro
which is cooler than cool. My mom
loaned me some earrings too. I wish
I could get a makeover on one of
those TV shows though, don't you?

Speaking of makeovers, my mom has
been acting mighty odd 18ly. She's
getting all dressed up and going out
and I have this sinking feeling
about it. Is she dating again?

BTW: I was just surfing around and
```

wondered if u saw all the new
features on bigfishbowl 18ly? I feel
like we picked the kewlest site to
join. All my friends are on it now
2. What about u? Let me know what u
think of all their new features.

Yours till the polka dots,

Maddie

Would that get Bigwheels to admit to something?

Midway through writing the message, Madison
had decided it was smarter not use the word blog or
mention Bloggerfishbowl by name. Madison didn't
want to sound like a snoop or anything. She wanted—
she *needed*—Bigwheels to be the one to tell her
what was going on, without any prompting. She
wanted to give Bigwheels a chance to be honest
first.

With fingers crossed, Madison pressed SEND.

Chapter 5

"Ivy Daly is dating a college sophomore?" Chet said.

He was sitting with the gang at the orange lunch table toward the back of the cafeteria. The rumors about Ivy's relationship with the Dunn Manor guy had become greatly exaggerated.

"College? What?" Egg cried. "Are you kidding me?"

Fiona nodded. At one point in the school year, she would have raced to defend even Ivy Daly from the spiraling gossip that could happen at school. But today Fiona was a party to all of it.

"I heard it from Aimee, who heard it from her brother," Fiona explained.

"Right," Aimee agreed. "But he's in high school, not college, Chet. Duh."

"Whatever," Chet grumbled. "Who cares about Ivy, anyway?"

"We do," Aimee said. "She's always talking about us."

Madison picked at the food on her plate, moving a pea from one side to the other without touching the potatoes in the middle. She didn't know what to say or think about Ivy anymore. Right now everything seemed different. Madison wasn't sure what was going on.

Linsday pulled up to the table with her tray and got in on the conversation. Apparently she had heard even more information about Ivy than Aimee had.

"I heard that Ivy went to Dunn Manor after school last week," Lindsay said softly. "I wonder what that means."

"Huh?" Madison's head shot up. "Do you think she went to meet that guy?"

"Yeah, maybe," Aimee said. "My brother told me that half the guys in his class saw Ivy making out with him."

"Come on . . ." Madison said. "Making out? At the school?"

"You guys!" Drew said. "Leave her alone, for goodness' sake."

"Who are you, her boyfriend?" Egg taunted Drew.

Madison smiled. Drew was sometimes the shy one, sometimes the silly one, but occasionally the voice of reason. A lot of times he got sucked in to

Egg's craziness, but he also knew when to stand up for his own opinions. Madison liked that about him.

"Hey, everyone! What's going on?" Hart asked, joining the group.

"Look, I'm not her boyfriend . . ." Drew said. "But he is."

Drew pointed directly at Hart.

"Me? Who? What are you jokers talking about? Whose boyfriend?" Hart stammered.

The table erupted with laughter—except for Madison. She had finally gotten to a place where she was secure in the knowledge that Ivy posed no romantic threat to her crush on Hart. But here was everyone else, still teasing Hart about Ivy's being his girlfriend, and laughing about it. Laughing!

Madison wanted to slink under the table and go *poof* in person—the same way she was able to go *poof* online.

The truth was, however, that everyone at the table was laughing at what was *behind* Madison. Across the lunchroom, Poison Ivy had suddenly stood up from her table when a carton of milk spilled on her shirt. She looked angry.

"Uh-oh. The enemy's in trouble," Aimee quietly joked.

"Yeah, someone go tell her not to cry over spilled milk," Egg added.

Everyone laughed even louder— this time including Madison, now that she knew what was going on.

From out of his backpack, Chet pulled a plastic container. Mrs. Waters had baked pumpkin cookies for everyone. Among their group of friends, Chet and Fiona's mother was known as the Cookie Queen.

Egg grabbed a handful of cookies and started to chomp. The rest of the group grabbed handfuls, too. Madison bit into one with a jagged edge and frosting, and savored the sweet flavors. She liked things that smelled and tasted like fall. It was one of her favorite times of the year.

"Did you guys work on the third journaling assignment?" Drew asked. Madison was relieved that he'd changed the subject.

"I did," Madison answered quickly. "It was a better task than yesterday. I didn't love writing about a scar."

"A scar? What was that? In our class, I don't think Mrs. Quill has been going in the right order of journaling assignments," Aimee said. "Did everyone have to make a list last night?"

Fiona opened her backpack, pulled out a black notebook, and pointed to the most recent entry. "Yup," she said. "Here's mine."

Madison looked around the table. She'd been keeping files and folders forever, but now all of her friends were writing, too. A part of her thought that that was a great thing—and another part of her wondered if it meant that now everyone would be muscling in on the things that she liked to do. It was fun to share interests—but was this too much?

Everyone's notebooks looked very much the same. Each student had added a personal touch. The front of Madison's was colored in parts where she'd doodled with an orange marker over white spaces. Ivy's had the princess sticker. Fiona had wrapped a blue rubber band around hers to keep the pages pressed tight.

Fiona plucked the blue band and read her assignment aloud.

Journaling #3
Topic: List twenty details about someone you
     know. Try to include details that are about
     more than just physical appearance.

"Yeah, I have the same one. I think we all have the same assignment," Drew said.

Chet, Egg, and Hart nodded knowingly.

"So, who wants to read first?" Aimee asked.

"Maddie's the best writer," Egg said. "Let's hear what she wrote first."

"Me? Why me?" Madison wheezed. She felt her stomach flip-flop. "I d—d—don't know what I wrote. . . ."

Of course, Madison *did* remember what she had written down. She just couldn't say it out loud.
    Hart.

"Come on, Maddie," Fiona insisted. "Read us your

entry first, and then we'll all read ours afterward."

Madison gritted her teeth. How could she possibly read hers aloud when Hart was sitting right there? They would guess right away whom she was referring to. Even worse, *he* would guess.

A crackle came up over the school announcement system. Madison breathed a sigh of relief. Everyone became distracted by a two-minute speech about school organization and discipline.

"In closing, please be sure to keep your locker combinations and your computer passwords in a safe place," Principal Bernard said at the end. Unwittingly he'd saved Madison's skin—or at least saved her from tumbling into a deep, dark hole of embarrassment.

"Someone tell me. What was that speech about?" Hart asked when Principal Bernard had finished.

"Yeah. What *was* that about?" Chet added.

"Am I crazy, or does our principal make no sense most of the time?" Aimee asked.

"Okay, here's what I wrote," Egg said, cutting the others off. He had pulled his black-and-white notebook out of his bag and opened to the assignment in question. "Who can guess who I'm writing about?" he asked. He showed them a list he'd written.

```
1. Blue hair
2. Nose pierced
```

3. Bent ears
4. Ripped jeans
5. Takes pictures

"That's Mariah!" Fiona piped up. Mariah Diaz was Egg's older sister and a ninth grader at their school.

"Of course Fiona knew that," Chet whined.

Egg smiled. Obviously, Fiona knew a lot about him and his family. She'd learned all the important stuff since they had started going out.

Madison could tell that Egg liked that. Lately, the pair didn't seem to mind showing a little bit of affection in public, either.

"What did you mean, Mariah has bent ears?" Madison asked.

"I don't know," Egg replied. "She has this one ear that looks bent. It's dented or something from this time when we went hiking and she fell over. . . ."

Chet laughed hard. Drew joined in. Soon all the boys were laughing and snorting about bent ears.

Fiona waved her hands to get everyone's attention. "Let me read mine next," she said.

Twenty Details
1. Likes to go online
2. Good with computers
3. Funny
4. Bad at keeping secrets

As she listened to Fiona's list, Madison's mind drifted to thoughts of her keypal. Fiona's list sounded like Bigwheels! Madison's keypal also liked to go online, was good with computers, and was funny. As far as keeping secrets, however, Bigwheels was great, not bad.

Madison thought about the e-mail she'd sent the night before asking Bigwheels to talk about the blog. She needed to know how Bigwheels could have left Madison out of such an important secret. How long would Madison have to wait before Bigwheels wrote back to tell her what was going on?

"Don't look now, but here comes Poison Ivy," Chet said.

Ivy Daly strolled up to the orange table with her drones, Rose and Joanie, who just stood there, staring. Ivy did all the talking, as usual.

"Excuse me," Ivy said with a snort.

No one wanted to respond at first. Then Aimee spoke up.

"May we help you?" Aimee asked.

Ivy flipped her red hair. "Not you. I wanted to talk to Madison," Ivy said.

"Well, I'm right here," Madison said gruffly. "So, talk."

"I need to talk to you about science class— alone." Ivy said. She clutched her books to her chest, but Madison could still see the word *SUPER* on Ivy's long-sleeved T-shirt.

"What about class?" Madison asked.

"Oooh!" Chet hissed. "Here comes a catfight."

"Be quiet, Chet!" Fiona said as she whacked him on the head with her notebook. He winced.

"Madison, you have to help me with those problems for Mr. Danehy's class," Ivy said. "After all, we're partners."

Aimee snickered. "Yeah, right."

"What is *your* problem?" Ivy said. "Are you always this . . . rude?"

Egg laughed out loud at that comment. "*We're* rude?" he said.

"Ivy," Madison said, ignoring Egg's comment. "Let's just say that I'll see you in science. Maybe we can figure something out there and not here, in the middle of lunch, okay?"

"Whatever," Ivy said abruptly. She turned on her one-inch, stacked heels and walked out of the cafeteria, with her drones following.

"You know, Ivy looks kind of sick," Fiona said in a whisper.

"I think she looks hot," Chet said.

Egg and Drew laughed.

Madison didn't want to say anything out loud, although she wondered if Fiona was right. For someone who had written *My life is so perfect* in her journal, Ivy appeared to be anything but perfect today.

"You should have asked her about the Dunn

Manor dude," Aimee said to Madison. "What better person to confirm the gossip than Poison Ivy herself?"

"Totally!" Lindsay chimed in.

"I think you guys have completely lost it," Madison said. She stood, picked up her lunch tray, and headed back toward the school kitchen to drop off her dishes and trash.

Madison knew there really was something different about Ivy, but she couldn't put her finger on it. Was it that boy from Dunn Manor? Had something happened between them at the high school? After all, Ivy had been crying in the bathroom. Was there a connection?

As Hart, Chet, and Madison walked off toward Mr. Danehy's classroom together, a bell echoed in the hallway.

It was like an alarm clock going off.

Aimee was right.

Madison would resolve all of the rumors about Ivy herself.

And science class was the ideal place to do it.

Chapter 6

Hart and Chet gave each other a way-up high five when they saw a note tacked on the door of Mr. Danehy's science classroom.

"What's the big deal?" Madison asked. Then she read the note.

Attention, Students in Science Classes 7 and 8:
Mr. Danehy will not be in school today.
Please meet at the regular time in the library.
Mr. Books, the librarian, will pass out all assignments.
Thank you.

"Let's just skip it," Chet said.

Hart laughed. "Yeah, and let's skip town while we're at it."

The boys laughed.

Madison frowned. "Wait. This isn't a free period. Mr. Books will be taking attendance. We'll get in trouble."

"So?" Chet laughed. "Since when did you turn into the science-class police?"

"Good one!" Hart said and laughed again. But at the same time he gave Madison a light nudge that said, *Hey, lighten up, we're just kidding around.*

Of course, no one was serious about skipping. The three friends—along with the rest of the students in class, including Ivy and Rose—walked directly upstairs to the library and media center to report in to Mr. Books.

The Far Hills Junior High library was a sprawling room packed with shelves, books, computers, and desks, with rows of windows along some walls. Up here, everyone knew they had to obey the not-too-much-talking rule that Mr. Books enforced. Up here, students actually did work. It was a perfect spot to which to relocate classes.

Once everyone had congregated upstairs, Mr. Books directed the students as to where to sit. Madison had already scoped out her usual table in the back, near the computer monitors. Usually she sat there alone or with her BFFs, but today, she thought she and Chet and Hart might hang out there together. Maybe they'd get some homework done—or just write notes the whole time.

Unfortunately, Mr. Books wasn't in an agreeable mood. And he wasn't into the idea of free seating, either. Instead, he passed out a stack of copies that Mr. Danehy had prepared. They were sheets of new vocabulary words and multiple-choice questions.

Madison couldn't believe it.

"I know this is a little unusual, but Mr. Danehy made up a special quiz for you kids to do in his absence," Mr. Books said. "There are about thirty questions here, including definitions. Some answers can be found in your books. Some need to be researched a little. That's why you're here in the library. Mr. Danehy wanted you to team up and sit with lab partners, just as you would sit with them downstairs in his classroom."

Madison's shoulders drooped. *Sit with lab partners?* She glanced at Ivy, who wasn't looking very pleased with the arrangement herself. Of course she wanted to sit with her friend Rose, not with Madison.

Ivy's hand popped up in the air.

Mr. Books scarcely acknowledged it. "Don't bother asking for seating exceptions," he grumbled, looking at Ivy and a few others who had also raised their hands. "There will be none."

Madison and Ivy walked toward each other reluctantly.

"Should we just find a place to sit and get this over with?" Madison asked her enemy.

Ivy looked up at the ceiling. "If we have to," she said.

"There's a table over there," Madison said, pointing to the darkened area of the library, where she wanted to sit.

They shuffled over to a small green wooden table very close to the science section and sat down in two white chairs that looked like swiveling spaceship seats from the 1970s. Madison loved how the parts of the library had different moods. Some areas were light, some were dark. Some were old-fashioned, and some were more modern. Over the years, various pieces of furniture had been inherited by the library. The spaceship-chair area was one of Madison's favorites. It was secluded and cozy—a perfect place to pull out her laptop.

If only she didn't have to share the space with *her*, meaning Ivy, of course.

Hart and Chet and the other boys who were paired together sat clear across the room from Madison and the other girls. They made their way for the "mod" section of the media lab. There, they piled their book bags on the floor next to a metal table with shiny metal chairs beneath a wide, sunny window, through which light poured into the room.

Although Hart's being so far away meant there would be no obvious flirting during the period,

Madison wasn't discouraged. No distractions meant action—as far as schoolwork was concerned. Up here she wouldn't get bogged down with pretend work—for example, sitting through an entire period pretending to take notes and pretending to look things up when, in reality, nothing she wrote in her notebook would make any sense later.

"So," Ivy said loudly.

"Shhh," Madison scolded her. "We have to keep our voices down."

"What are you, the librarian's pet?" Ivy sneered. "I don't have to be quiet, and I definitely don't have to do what you tell me to do. . . ."

"Well, we *have* to do the assignment together," Madison said. "Maybe we should try to cooperate."

Ivy laughed. "You're not the boss of me."

"What are you talking about?" Madison said. Ivy sounded as if she were back in third grade.

"Is there a problem here?" Mr. Books asked. He appeared from nowhere, staring over the top of his glasses, which were perched on the bridge of his nose.

"Oh, no problem here," Ivy said with a flick of her wrist. "We were just getting ready to sit down. We have loads of work to do, and we want to get right to it. Don't we, Maddie?"

Madison wanted to wipe Ivy's smile right off her face. *She* was the real librarian's pet. And it was grosser than gross watching her in action.

They finally sat down and took out their science books. The quiz, as it turned out, was super easy. Normally, Mr. Danehy's assignments (and pop quizzes) were marathon study adventures. But, working together, Madison and Ivy actually got the thirty questions completed in almost no time.

That left half a period with nothing to do—and nowhere to go. Mr. Books had said that anyone who finished early had to remain seated. His exact words had been: *"Use your time wisely, students, and don't fritter."*

Madison wasn't sure she knew what *fritter* even meant.

Without consulting Madison on what to do next, Ivy pulled out her princess composition book and a red pen. Madison could see the initials *I.R.D.* on the side of the pen. *I* was for Ivy, of course. *D* was for Daly. But for some reason, Madison couldn't remember what the *R* stood for. It felt weird not to remember something important about someone who had been a friend once. Then again, becoming sworn enemies had caused Madison to forget as much as possible about Ivy.

"What's the *R* stand for again?" Madison asked.

"Huh?" Ivy snorted. "Oh, wow. Are you staring at me again?"

"I only asked a question," Madison said. "I wasn't staring at you. I just saw your pen. . . ."

"The *R* stands for *Renee*," Ivy snarled. "After my grandmother. Remember?"

"Oh, yeah," Madison said, nodding.

She did remember. Ivy's grandmother, Renee Daly, had been a teen beauty queen back in the 1950s. Ivy had inherited all of her trophies and one tarnished tiara that she kept in a box in her room. Ivy probably thought winning pageants was genetic. That explained the fixation on wardrobe and hair and being the starlet of seventh grade.

"Gee, Maddie. I remember *your* middle name," Ivy said. "Francesca, right? Because your mom's name starts with an F—Francine. At least, that's what you told me a long time ago."

Madison almost fell off her chair in shock. How could Ivy have remembered all those facts about her middle name when Madison couldn't even remember the first letter of Ivy's middle name? Once again, Mr. Gibbons's advice rang true. The unexpected was to be expected—even as far as the enemy was concerned.

"What journal question are you working on?" Madison asked. "The one about the scar? The list of twenty things?"

"No," Ivy said curtly. "I did those already. Mr. Gibbons told me I could write whatever I wanted in between assignments. He gave me an extra list of questions to think about. That's what I'm writing."

Madison's heart sank. This was bad news.

"What do you mean he gave you an *extra* list?" Madison asked.

"He gave me a list of questions like 'Write about a time when someone made you a promise and broke it' and 'Describe a time when you saved someone from getting hurt.'"

"Wow, those are good questions," Madison said thoughtfully, although she couldn't begin to imagine what kind of answers superficial Ivy would write.

"Yeah, they are good questions, but it's hard to write about bad stuff sometimes, because things are just so good in my life, you know?" Ivy bragged.

The words Madison had seen inside Ivy's journal flashed into her thoughts once more: *My life is just so perfect.* Madison shuddered.

Miss Poison Ivy Renee Daly couldn't know a single thing about what it meant to feel embarrassed or sad or unliked, could she? It didn't seem fair that Mr. Gibbons had singled out the enemy for a special writing assignment.

Journals were Madison's territory, not Ivy's.

"Um . . . who else has this other list?" Madison asked quietly.

"I don't know. Just me, I think," Ivy said with a toss of her head. She gave Madison a *Just leave me alone* look, glanced back down at her composition book, and started to write once again.

"Wait a second!" Madison interrupted Ivy's writing. "Wait. I want the list, too. Give me the list."

"Ask Mr. Gibbons for it," Ivy replied.

"I was thinking that maybe you could share some of the questions with me," Madison suggested.

Ivy shot Madison a cruel, piercing look. "Share? Ha!" Ivy said. "You're kidding me, right?"

"What do you mean, 'kidding'?" Madison replied. "No, I'm not kidding. Show me some of the questions."

All of a sudden, Ivy burst into laughter that was loud enough to draw Mr. Books's attention back to their table. He'd heard them clear across the library.

"Shhhh!" he cautioned as he approached their table, his finger up to his lips. After standing guard for about five minutes near their small library table, he disappeared across the room.

"So now you know how I feel, Maddie," Ivy said. "Like, you never share science notes with me—so I'm not sharing English questions with you. Besides, these journals are private, aren't they? What's mine is mine."

Madison felt like a teakettle that was just starting to boil. But she could not, under any circumstances, blow her top. If Madison's voice got too loud, that would raise another red flag for Mr. Books, and she did not, under any circumstances, want to end up in Principal Bernard's office.

Madison bit her tongue so she wouldn't invite trouble. She stared at the enemy, wondering what the next move should be.

Ivy looked like a mannequin, sitting in her chair

with her legs crossed under the table. She wore red Mary Janes and a flowered skirt and top that Madison had seen in a recent e-mail advertisement from the Boop-Dee-Doop catalog. Around her neck on a beaded choker, Ivy wore a heart-shaped charm. It looked as though she might have gotten her red hair highlighted with streaks of—was that auburn? And there wasn't a strand out of place. Not only was Ivy's life perfect on the inside—Ivy looked perfect on the outside.

Even though she told herself not to look, Madison's eyes wandered from Ivy's outfit and hair to the pages of Ivy's journal.

Ivy had written down a new topic at the top of the page. It was a topic that Madison had never seen before. It must have been from Mr. Gibbons's special list of questions.

> Write about a time you had to wait for something you wanted.
> What's the point of writing about this? I am supposed to see M. and H. as soon as possible but I don't know what will happen. J. didn't have happy

Madison shifted in her chair.
M.? H.?
Madison? Hart?
Who else could it be? And *who* was *J.*?

"Um . . . Ivy?" Madison asked.

Ivy looked over at Madison with her wide blue eyes. She blinked once, then a second time. Ivy wasn't wearing her usual mascara and eyeliner. In fact, she had no makeup on at all. She looked like a different person.

"What is it?" Ivy rolled her eyes emphatically and let out an enormous sigh. "Do you have a problem?"

"Not me."

"Then bug off. Mr. Books will come back if you don't."

Madison shifted again in her chair, and her green T-shirt with the palm tree and stars on the front rode up. (The shirt didn't fit quite right, unlike Ivy's red top with the little bow neckline, which fit Ivy *perfectly*.) Madison pulled the shirt down and tried tucking it into her jeans, but the waist on the jeans was a super-low-rider style, so nothing stayed tucked. It was bad enough to deal with Ivy's snarly attitude. Now Madison's clothes were completely malfunctioning.

"Look," Ivy said. "Why can't you just write in your journal, and I'll write in mine, okay? That is . . . *if* you have anything interesting to say."

There was no good response to Ivy's final comment. All Madison could do was sit there, open her own notebook, absentmindedly roll her pen between her fingers, look pensive, and pretend Ivy's barbs didn't sting.

But they did sting, a lot, even after all those years of being enemies with Ivy.

They stung so much that Madison couldn't write anything down. She stared at an empty, white, lined page in her journal for ten full minutes without writing a single word. And by that time, the period was over.

On the walk home that afternoon, the streets and sidewalks seemed emptier than empty. Madison felt empty, too, although she wasn't sure why. There was a hollow pang left over from the science class study hall and Poison Ivy's venomous comments, but that wasn't the whole reason.

Was it because her BFFs were all elsewhere? Fiona had an after-school meeting with the photography club; Aimee had dance; and Egg and the guys were over at Chet and Fiona's house playing Disaster Zone (since Mr. Waters had finally gotten the family PC fixed).

Madison didn't know.

Upon reaching her porch, Madison opened the screen door to find Phin curled up under the table in the hall. Normally, Phinnie would rush the door and lick Madison all over with happy-dog kisses. But today he just snored. Madison tiptoed past him into the kitchen.

The basement door was wide open.

"Mom? Are you down there?" Madison asked.

"Hello, honey bear," Mom yelled up. She came to

the bottom of the stairs wearing rubber gloves and a ratty T-shirt. "I needed to get my mind off work and some other things," Mom continued, "so I thought I'd finally clean up this mess down here. You know, there are file cabinets down here with loads of your collages and other stuff. You haven't looked at those in ages."

"I know," Madison said wistfully. Before Dad got her a laptop, Madison had spent lots of time typing on their old computer, tearing up magazines, and doing other things down in the Finn basement. She used to play "school" with only herself as both teacher and students, and she still had the make-believe tests to show for it. Each "student" had special handwriting and special habits; for example, Jorge was a lousy speller, and Emerson liked to draw smiley faces over all of her letter *I*'s. There were so many happy memories of teaching down in that basement that, despite Mom's pleas, Madison knew it would be impossible for her to clean up or throw anything out from her file cabinets and shelves.

"I'll deal with it later," she told Mom abruptly.

"Okay, then," Mom called back. "I'll be up in an hour and we can decide on dinner. I have taco mix, broccoli, and tofu tonight."

Madison grimaced. A few years back Mom had gone vegetarian, thanks to the influence of Aimee's mom, who always prepared macrobiotic meals. Madison still wasn't too happy about the switch to vegetarianism, even though she knew it was the healthier way.

After tossing her bag onto the kitchen table, Madison opened her laptop. While it booted up, Madison opened up a container of strawberry yogurt and spooned it into a bowl along with some honey granola and raisins. If she was forced to eat tofu later, she needed a decent snack now.

Madison's laptop beeped with e-mail.

"Yeah!" she shrieked. It was the one she'd been waiting for.

```
From: Bigwheels
To: MadFinn
Subject: Re: Bigfishbowl
Date: Wed 13 Oct 4:10 PM
```
Thanks for your e-mail & sorry I haven't written back but I've had 3 MAJOR tests on Monday and Tuesday and I'm only now checking my mailbox. I'm in school, in the computer lab and I'm blowing off my HW so--don't tell anyone! *>)

You know I think we should write in to one of those shows where two people get made over TOGETHER. How cool would that b?

BTW yes I have been on bigfishbowl

a lot 18ly and I'm guessing
(is it keypal ESP?) that you are
talking about the new feature
BLOGGERFISHBOWL aka BFB. Um . . . did
u find my blog there? I knew you
would--!!!:>) And I know I should
have said something b4 but I wasn't
sure what to say exactly. I mean ur
like my BFF online and normally I'd
spill and tell u everything but I
just can't this time. Not yet.
Sorry.

Pleasepleaseplease WBS.

Yours till the lily pads (we did
virtual frog dissections last
week!).

Vicki aka Bigwheels

Madison swallowed a few more spoonfuls of
yogurt and granola as she scanned Bigwheels's
e-mail again. But no matter how many times she
reread the words, Madison couldn't accept it.
Bigwheels had a BIG secret?
Madison needed to find out exactly what it was.
Soon.

78

Chapter 7

From: MadFinn
To: Bigwheels
Subject: Re: Re: Bigfishbowl
Date: Thurs 14 Oct 11:20 AM

Now I'm the one in the media lab @
school writing 2 u! Thanks 4 ur
e-mail. Is everything ok? U sound
different. I know u said u couldn't
talk about it but I wanted to make
sure u know that u can always
ALWAYS keep it real w/me. Really. I
consider u 2 be 1 of my BFs of
course even tho ur all the way
across the USA. So . . .

We have this weird project in
school. We're keeping journals. It
sounds like my kind of thing but
for some reason I am NOT feeling
inspired. Un42n8ly Poison Ivy
obviously IS inspired b/c she keeps
writing (and talking) about how
absolutely PERFECT her life is. She
has to be THE most plastic person
on the planet.

Well, I have to get ready 4 class
so I better go.

Ur turn to WBS.

Yours till the book reports,

Maddie

Brrrrinnnnnnnnnnnnnng.
Upon hearing the class bell ring, Madison clicked
SEND, powered down her laptop, and stuffed all of
her books, including her journaling notebook, and
her laptop back into her orange bag. Although the
bag was bursting at the seams, she heaved it over
her shoulder and raced out of the media lab, taking
two steps at a time down to the next class.

At the bottom of the staircase, Madison took a
corner too fast, and the weight of her bag pulled her
in the wrong direction.

Wham!

She slammed into someone coming from the opposite direction. Her bag dragged her to the ground. Everything inside spilled onto the floor and the other person's books went tumbling, too.

"Finnster?"

Madison looked up and saw Hart looking down at her. He was rubbing his shoulder.

"Ouch. Your book bag attacked me," he said. "What's in there?"

Madison realized that both his and her stuff was everywhere: her laptop, his wallet, and lots of papers were scattered on the ground. Other kids stepped around the crash site. Kneeling down, she scrambled to get her hands on as much as she could without having her fingers stomped on.

"I'm such a klutz," Madison said, pausing to put her head in her hands. "I can't believe I whammed into you like that. I am SO sorry. And now look at this mess. . . ."

Hart laughed. He kneeled down to retrieve his own books and wallet and to help her pick up her papers. "My dad would call this a happy accident. He always says profound things like that."

"Huh?" Madison blurted out. She felt a blush coming on. Hart was definitely flirting again. *Definitely.* She could see it in his eyes this time. He never stopped smiling.

Madison continued to try to gather the items

that had flown out of her bag. As Hart handed Madison a stack of loose-leaf paper, she grabbed her science notebook and a few stray pens.

"I think your laptop survived," Hart said.

"Thanks," Madison sighed. "I don't know what I would do if my laptop was injured."

"You could take it to a laptop hospital," Hart said.

"Bah-dum ching!" Madison joked. "Gee, Hart, you should be a comedian," she added, in her most sarcastic voice. Now she was really flirting, too.

"Is this yours?" Hart asked, holding up Madison's black-and-white composition notebook from Mr. Gibbons's class.

Madison gasped. Her journal! The way Hart was holding it she could see a couple of the pages folded over. What did those pages say? Madison strained to peek.

"I'll take that!" she cried in a sudden burst of paranoia, grabbing the journal right out of Hart's hands. One of the pages was completely exposed. Right there in black and white was written the name Madison Jones.

Had Hart seen that or any of the other dozens of name combinations scribbled in the same margin? That question put her tummy into instant knots. Madison was sweating just thinking about it.

Gulp.

With her notebook still clutched tightly to her

side, Madison wished Hart a speedy good-bye. Of course, he wasn't ready to go.

"So, have you been writing more?" Hart asked, indicating the notebook. "Do you like the journal project?"

"Um . . . um . . . huh?" Madison stammered. She couldn't look him in the eyes.

"Are you heading to science?" Hart asked easily, checking his watch. "I hear Mr. Danehy is back."

"I heard that, too," Madison said. "If you're going to class, why are you walking in this direction?"

Hart tossed his head. "I was going to drop something off . . . but I haven't got time now."

"Sorry," Madison said. "My fault."

"No prob," Hart said. He smiled.

Madison wanted to smile, too, but she couldn't. All she could think about was the journal, still tucked tightly under her armpit. With each passing moment she was becoming more and more convinced that of course Hart had seen the doodles, seen "Madison Jones," and was right now planning a breakup with her. Of course, that would have made a lot more sense if he had actually been going out with her, but just the same—the gut-wrenching, embarrassing, and ghastly emotions were still there, all rolled into one.

Naturally, Hart didn't say anything more about the book, which left Madison guessing all the way to science class.

At least Mr. Danehy was back—and feeling much better. He hardly even sniffled anymore. Not having to go back upstairs to Mr. Books was a huge relief.

Madison and Hart separated to take their seats at opposite ends of the lab. Madison went to her spot near Ivy.

"This seat is taken," Ivy said as Madison approached.

"Taken? By who?" Madison asked.

"By you, twit," Ivy said with a smirk.

"Oh, like, that's funny," Madison said. She climbed onto the lab stool and placed her journal on the countertop.

"Is that your journal for school?" Ivy asked.

"You know it is," Madison nodded. "Where's yours?"

"In a safe place," Ivy said. "I don't want anyone looking at it. Not that there's much to read. I mean, life couldn't be better right now, you know?"

"I bet," Madison said, vaguely annoyed. Silently, she wished a curse on Ivy and Ivy's journal. If she had to hear one more word about how perfect the world of Ivy Daly was, Madison was going to be sick!

After school, Madison couldn't wait to complain to her BFFs about Ivy, who was getting on everyone's last nerve. Plus, according to Aimee, there were more Ivy rumors circulating.

They decided to chat online after school. Aimee,

Fiona, and Madison arranged to meet in a chat room called BFFTOGO. Madison was always trying to find chat rooms with the cleverest names.

```
<BalletGrl>: Sry but PI is awful
<MadFinn>: IDK if she realizes
   it tho and how PATHETIC is
   she????
<Wetwinz>: remember when I thought
   she used to be sooo nice???
<BalletGrl>: yeah b4 her heart
   transplant ha ha
<Wetwinz>: Hart transplant?
<MadFinn>: LOL u guys r funny 2day
   aren't u?
<BalletGrl>: So ppl this is what I
   know. The guy @ Dunn Manor's name
   is TA DA! Fred.
<MadFinn>: Fred?
<BalletGrl>: well that's what doug
   told me
<Wetwinz>: LOL I know hes ur bro
   but is he a reliable source or is
   he good at making stuff up b/c MY
   bro makes up weird lies ATT!
<MadFinn>: u know aim I'm sry 2 but
   ivy would NEVER date a Fred guy
   would she?
<BalletGrl>: yeah maybe not
<MadFinn>: !!!<>)?
<BalletGrl>: the guy Ivy is seeing
```

is like the loser of tenth grade like he got suspended once for doing drugs

<MadFinn>: maybe this means Ivy will get in trouble 2--that would be rich! For some reason I am madder than mad @ her 2day

<Wetwinz>: come on ur mad @ her evry day, Maddie

<BalletGrl>: yah

<MadFinn>: well aren't u? Aren't u sick of the whole look-at-me-I'm-so-pretty-and-perfect-and-every-one-should-worship-me thing she has going?

<BalletGrl>: hey doug just got home want me to ask about the Fred thing maybe he knows more?

<Wetwinz>: Nah I have 2 go do homework b4 we go 2 dinner we're eating out 2nite

<MadFinn>: wait--have u guys written in ur journal yet today?

<BalletGrl>: almost done! I always try 2 finish the question in my study lab

<Wetwinz>: sort of done--I jotted down a few ideas. What was the question again?

<MadFinn>: Write a desc. of someone u know

```
<BalletGrl>: it's a lot like
  yesterday
<Wetwinz>: yeah but more paragraphs
  and not list
<BalletGrl>: I better finish mine
<MadFinn>: Me 2 BYE TTYL
<BalletGrl>: *poof*
<Wetwinz>: *poof*
```

Madison wondered where Ivy was right at that very moment—and if she was working on her journal—or just basking in the perfectness of her own life.

She felt all the ugly anger toward her enemy building up again inside. She didn't feel much like writing anything nice, so she tried scribbling a description of Poison Ivy in the pages of her notebook.

Description

How do you describe someone you hate? Let me try. Miss Perfect thinks she is so great, but her big head is covered with red hair like flames shooting everywhere. She looks through you when you talk to her, like she can see all your weaknesses and she can't wait to tell you off. And she <u>always</u> has something mean to say.

87

Madison stopped writing. Now *she* was the one saying the mean things.

"Maddie! Are you online?" Mom cried from downstairs. "Can I borrow your laptop? My computer down here isn't working right, and I just need to check something online fast."

"Sure, Mom!"

Madison trotted downstairs with her laptop and the portable disk drive.

"Mom, can I ask you something?" Madison asked as she curled up in a ball on the large chair in Mom's office.

"Yes?" Mom replied.

"What am I supposed to do about Ivy? Because I can't deal anymore," Madison said.

"Deal with what?"

"I cannot deal with anything Poison Ivy says or does!" Madison said.

Mom made a face. "So? Is there anything you can do about it?"

"I want to request that I switch lab partners in science—and maybe even get a different home-room so I don't have to see Ivy every single morning. Is that possible? Can't you write me a note or something?"

"Maddie . . . of course I can't," Mom said.

"But I hate her, Mom," Madison said with a scowl. "I hate and detest and despise her and her perfect, perfect life."

"*Hate* is a very strong word," Mom replied. "Who says her life is perfect?"

"She does!"

Madison told her mom what she'd seen, by mistake, of course, in Ivy's journal and what Ivy had told her in class.

"She's acting snootier than ever, and it just makes me want to SCREAM. Today she called me a twit! Plus, there are these rumors . . . well, I can't confirm anything, but apparently she's dating some guy . . . and he's older than us. . . ."

"Older?" Mom asked. "Dating?"

"Aimee's brother says the guy is a sophomore at Dunn Manor."

"Oh, boy," Mom said.

"Mom, I even saw Ivy crying in the girls' room at school. She is *such* a total drama queen."

Mom clasped her hands in front of her.

She got very quiet.

"Maddie," Mom said, "I think there's something you need to know."

Chapter 8

"Why are you acting so serious?" Madison asked Mom. "You're making me nervous."

Mom put her hand on Madison's arm. "I need to tell you something important. It's a secret, but I'm going to share it with you. Can you keep this a secret? You can't tell anyone right now. Not even Aimee and Fiona."

Madison listened carefully as Mom spoke.

"When you were younger, I was very good friends with Ivy's mother, as you know," Mom said.

"So?" Madison couldn't keep herself from interrupting. "What does that have to do with any-thing?"

"So . . . I haven't seen or talked to Ivy's mom

in ages. We keep in touch a little through e-mails, but that's about it. She's been quite busy these past few years. . . ."

"Mom, what's your point?" Madison asked. The suspense was killing her.

"My point is that Ivy's mother happened to be at Salon Pink at the same time as me the other day— and we started talking."

"About Ivy?" Madison asked, intrigued.

Mom shook her head. "Maddie, just listen."

Madison sat back in her seat and crossed her arms. "Okay, okay."

"So, I got to talking with Ivy's mom and . . . well . . . apparently she's sick."

"Ivy's sick?"

"No, Maddie. Mrs. Daly is sick."

"Oh," Madison said. "How sick?"

"She was diagnosed with breast cancer a month ago."

Madison's entire body went limp. "Cancer?"

"Come here," Mom said. She held her arms out to Madison.

Madison walked into her mother's arms and squeezed her tightly around the middle. She thought about all the things Aimee had said when she told Madison that her dance teacher had been diagnosed with cancer. Aimee had said that learning that news felt like getting a punch in the stomach. That's what Madison felt like, too, right now.

"Is it bad?" Madison asked.

"From what I understand," Mom went on, "Mrs. Daly said they caught it early, so it seems like she has a good chance of a full recovery. But she's undergoing some medical treatments now."

"Chemotherapy?" Madison asked. She knew about that from science class and television.

"I think that chemo is part of her treatment, yes," Mom answered. "Unfortunately, Mrs. Daly has been suffering some side effects that aren't too pleasant. She's losing her hair. That's why she was at the salon—to get her head shaved."

"But her hair will grow back, right? She'll get better soon, right?"

"She won't know if the cancer is gone until she has had all the treatments. And that takes some time. But for now she's hoping for the best."

"Poor Ivy," Madison said. She felt her chest start to heave a little, a wave of emotion building inside her.

"Exactly," Mom said. "Ivy must be going through a lot right now."

"So maybe that's why she's . . ." Madison stopped in midsentence. "Oh, Mom, I can't believe I said all of those things about her."

"Well, I know you and Ivy haven't been friends for some time," Mom said. "It's understandable. We all say things we don't mean sometimes."

"But wait a minute. . . ." Madison said, her whole

face lighting up with a bright idea. "If her mom is so sick, then why is Ivy writing in her journal about how perfect her life is?"

"Sometimes when life is not so perfect, it's nice to pretend that things are better. Maybe she feels she needs to put on a brave front," Mom said with a shrug. "Only Ivy can answer that question, Maddie. Perhaps you should speak to her about it."

"Yeah, right," Madison said.

Mom frowned. "Madison Francesca Finn . . ." she said in that voice that she used when she was disappointed or upset.

"I know," Madison said. "I really should be more considerate."

Mom nodded. "Don't you think Ivy would do the same for you?"

Madison raised an eyebrow. "Um . . . is that a trick question?"

"Well," Mom said, "you get my point."

They talked for a few more minutes about cancer and what it meant to get radiation treatments and how hard life at the Daly house must be right then. Madison began to feel worse and worse about all the nasty things she'd written in her journal. She thought back to the entries that she'd spied in Ivy's journal, in particular the page that had the initials *M.*, *H.*, and *J.* on it. Madison realized that those letters probably never stood for Madison or anyone else in their class at all. That *M* must have been for "Mom" and the *J* for Ivy's older sister, Janet.

"You know, Maddie," Mom said, "everyone has different ways of coping with change and stressful situations. Maybe Ivy's journal is the one place where she can really express herself right now. Isn't that what you do in your files?"

"Yes, but that's different," Madison said.

"How?" Mom asked.

Madison didn't have an answer. She shifted the subject.

"What about Ivy dating a high-school sophomore?" Madison asked. "Don't you think that is weird?"

"Oh, Maddie," Mom said with a shake of her head. "I think you'd better check your facts before you go spreading rumors. I do know from Mrs. Daly that Ivy has been spending time with a high-school boy from Dunn Manor. . . ."

"Aha!" Madison said.

"But it's not because they're dating. It's because the boy's mother is also sick. Mrs. Daly told me that Ivy and he met each other at a Far Hills Hospital cancer support group. There are about five or six kids in the area who know each other from the group."

"Why is she keeping everything a secret?" Madison asked.

Mom shrugged. "Embarrassed? Afraid? I can think of a lot of good reasons not to talk about it."

Madison wondered what she would do if she were the one with the sick mother.

"Rowwowoorrroooooo!"

From across the room, Phinnie came running toward Madison for no reason. His little claws click-clacked on the polished floor, and then he slid right over to Madison's shoes.

"Hello, Phinnie," Madison said as she scooped him up.

Mom put on the kettle. "Do you want some tea?" she asked Madison. "I can make a pot of chamomile."

Madison shook her head. "No tea for me, Mom." She poured herself a glass of root beer instead.

"You know," Mom said as they sat sipping their hot and cold drinks together. "Maybe you should do something nice for Ivy."

"Nice? Are you kidding?" Madison cried.

Mom frowned again. "Madison Francesca Finn . . ."

"Why should I do something nice for *her*?" Madison replied.

"Just because," Mom said, "it's the right thing to do." She took her teacup and grabbed two newspapers off the table. Then she kissed Madison lightly on the forehead.

"I know you'll do the right thing," Mom said to Madison before walking out of the room.

Madison stared up at the kitchen clock. The day had flown by. A lot could happen in one afternoon, she mused. One minute everything seemed clear, and the next minute everything seemed so fuzzy.

That was how Madison felt right now.

Fuzzy.

She couldn't do something nice for Ivy. No way! Aimee and Fiona would think that Madison had lost it. And what would the drones think?

Madison left the kitchen, laptop in one hand and glass of root beer in the other. She marched upstairs with Phinnie.

What would Bigwheels do in a situation like this?

Madison logged on to bigfishbowl.com to see if her keypal was online.

She wasn't.

Then Madison checked her e-mailbox to see if Bigwheels had sent any e-mails since the previous day.

She hadn't.

Finally, Madison went onto Bloggerfishbowl to see if she could locate Bigwheels's blog. She scanned the list of names and found it.

```
Don't Ask: The Whole Truth
A blog by Vicki (aka Bigwheels)
```

Madison clicked on the icon to enter the blog. But when the home page appeared, there was no new information. Bigwheels had not added any entries since the last time Madison had visited.

The whole truth? Madison said to herself, rereading the name of Bigwheels's blog. That's not true at all.

The phone rang, and Madison paused to see if maybe the phone was for her. But when her mom didn't call her, she turned back to her monitor. Even up in her room, Madison could hear Mom laugh and say, "Oh, it's you!"

Who was she talking to?

Madison returned to her monitor again. With no new facts about Bigwheels or her big secret, she signed out of the Web site and went into her personal files instead.

 Keep It Real

Rude Awakening: When it comes to enemies and friends, I thought I saw the light. But noooo! I am totally in the dark.

Why are neither my enemy nor my keypal the people they seem to be? Am I that tuned out to what is really going on in everyone's life? Or am I just over-thinking everything again???

I can be so good at that.

"Maddie, I need you!" Mom cried from downstairs.

Madison ran downstairs and into the kitchen.

Mom was busy doing a few dishes that had been left in the sink. She looked stressed.

"That was someone on the phone from work," Mom explained. "I need to ask you a big favor. Tomorrow, can you go to your dad's after school instead of coming back here? I won't be home until late. He can drive you back after dinner if you want, or you can stay there. I know you're seeing him Sunday, too. . . ."

Madison didn't answer. She just stared at Mom in wide-eyed confusion.

"Well?" Mom asked.

"Why?" Madison asked.

"What do you mean, 'why'? I just told you," Mom said.

"What?"

"Madison . . ." Mom was getting testy at all the word games.

Madison stared silently. She wanted to say, "Mom, tell me the truth. What's going on? You've been sneaking around doing something and making me hang out with Dad a lot lately, and that *has* to mean something. . . ." But she didn't speak up. Not yet.

"Maddie, I think you have an active imagination," Mom said with a wide grin. "If I had something to tell you—I would."

"Fine," Madison said, even though she felt very *un*fine.

Mom was dressing up in fancy clothes, acting nervous and scattered, and taking strange phone calls.

In the pit of her stomach, Madison worried that Mom—like Bigwheels and like Ivy—was keeping a very big secret.

Chapter 9

On Friday morning, Madison's head felt like a wheel. It was spinning.

For one thing, she'd come to school in a super-grouchy mood. It was pouring outside, and her pants had gotten wet. After their conversation the night before, Mom and Madison had hardly spoken at breakfast that morning. As requested, and grudgingly, Madison would be heading to Dad's after school.

Madison walked into FHJH on the early side and headed for the lockers. She scanned the hallway searching for Aimee and Fiona, but they hadn't arrived yet. Madison plucked her books out of the locker and stuffed her orange bag with everything she needed for her classes. She took her time.

"Hello, Maddie," Mrs. Wing, Madison's computer teacher, said as she walked by.

"Hi, Mrs. Wing," Madison replied, briefly shaking off the sleepy, woozy fog inside her head. They talked about computer class and the school Web site. It had been a week since Madison had even set foot inside the computer lab.

"I really need your help early next week to update our Web site," Mrs. Wing said. "Can I count on you?"

Madison nodded. "Of course," she said.

"Egg and Drew and Lance will be coming, too," Mrs. Wing said.

Madison held back her laughter. Lance barely knew how to operate a computer, as far as she could tell. But he always volunteered for everything.

Egg and Drew, on the other hand, were like team leaders. They knew *everything*.

By the time Madison and Mrs. Wing had finished speaking, the morning sequence of bells had rung, and kids flooded the corridors. Everyone said their hurried good mornings and headed for their home-rooms.

"Fiona!" Madison cried when she saw her BFF.

"Maddie!" Fiona said. She came over and gave Madison a BFF squeeze. "Where were you last night? I tried calling you!"

Madison gave her a quizzical look. "You did? Oh, I guess I missed the call. Or maybe Mom forgot to tell me."

"Well, Mom and Dad got all this new software for our computer since Dad got the machine fixed. I wanted you to come over and see it. I guess it was a little bit late. Maybe you can come over today?"

"Can't," Madison said. "I have to go to my dad's."

"Didn't you already go to your dad's once this week?" Fiona asked.

Madison nodded. "I did, but . . . well . . . Mom has another date."

"Date?" Fiona's eyes lit up. "She has a boyfriend?"

"No," Madison said right away. "Well, I don't know, exactly. Maybe she does. . . . I've been thinking she does. . . . She's acting different. She says it's a business date, but I don't . . . I don't know if I believe her. . . ."

"A date! That is major news!" Fiona declared.

Aimee came over with her backpack still on her back. "Morning, everyone," she said with a smile.

"Aim, Maddie's mom has a date tonight," Fiona whispered.

"Really?" Aimee said. "Whoa."

"No!" Madison cried. "You guys . . . This is how rumors get started."

Fiona tried to convince Madison that she should

forget going to her dad's house after school that day. Instead, she should come to Fiona's and hang out until it was time to go home. Or maybe she could even sleep over?

"I guess I could check with my dad," Madison said.

"Yeah!" Aimee said. "Change your plans! You have to hang with us today, Maddie! And then tomorrow we're all going over to Egg's to work on his blog."

"Oh, yeah! I almost forgot!" Fiona said.

Madison looked at Fiona and then back at Aimee. She listened to their banter as if she were watching a tennis match. Why was this the first time she'd heard about any of this?

"So, is everyone going to Egg's house on Saturday?" Madison asked.

"I doubt it. It's a last-minute plan. Egg and Drew just decided last night, and Egg told me about it when we were sending Insta-Messages last night."

"Hart will be there. . . ." Fiona said with a grin.

"So will Ivy!" Aimee said.

"What?" Madison's face turned pale.

"I'm kidding, I'm kidding!" Aimee said. "Duh."

Madison told Fiona she'd check with her dad about changing the plans. Then she said good-bye and headed for her homeroom. Unfortunately, Madison and her BFFs had been assigned to different homerooms.

The halls thinned out as Madison walked along. She didn't see Egg anywhere. Because the home-rooms were organized alphabetically, Diaz and Finn were in the same one. Madison wanted to find him and ask why she had been the last one in their group to find out about the Saturday get-together.

Madison kept her eyes peeled for Ivy, too, since she was also a *D* (for Daly). All morning long, in the back of her mind, Madison had been rehearsing exactly the right thing to say when she saw Ivy. She needed a way to bring up the subject of mothers . . . or getting sick . . . or something. Was that possible to do without sounding too forced? Would Ivy ever tell Madison what was really going on in her life—would she peel back the perfect veneer that she'd used in her journal?

Homeroom was chaos. Almost no one was sitting down. A cluster of kids stood by the windowsill watching the rain. It was pouring.

Madison sat at the table with the other kids and waited for the final bell to ring. She didn't take her eyes off the front door of the classroom.

"Hi."

"Hi."

"Hi."

Madison said her good mornings to all of the familiar faces: Hilary Klein, dressed in matching col-ors, as usual; Fiona's soccer buddy, Daisy Espinoza; and, of course, Lindsay Frost, who was really one of her BFFs—and way more than just a basic friend-friend.

Poison Ivy Renee Daly did not appear.

Madison was perplexed. Where had the enemy gone? Now that Madison knew the real deal about Ivy and her mother, she hoped that Ivy would talk about it a little. It seemed unlikely that she'd spill all the beans, but Madison was willing to settle for any information she could get.

And so, here was Madison . . . ready to talk . . . while Ivy was missing.

The homeroom dismissal bell rang, and kids walked off to their first classes. Madison headed to Mr. Gibbons's room. Maybe Ivy was late for school and Madison would see her in English class instead? That sounded right.

But Ivy did not appear in Mr. Gibbons's class, either.

Why was Ivy absent? Had something happened to Mrs. Daly?

Mr. Gibbons stepped up to the board and wrote out the journaling assignment for the weekend.

Journaling #6
Topic: Write about something you have lost.

"That's it?" a kid called out from the back row.

Mr. Gibbons raised his eyebrows. "Deceptively simple, I'd say."

Madison traced circles in the margins near where she'd written down the topic. Doodling was a good way of thinking through things. Then she realized she was doodling more than just shapes. She'd doodled a name.

Ivy.

Madison quickly crossed out the name and sat up straight in her chair.

But it was very clear.

Madison had lost Ivy somewhere along the way. And it bothered her. And right now, at that very moment, in the middle of seventh-grade English class, Madison Francesca Finn was worried about her long-lost friend—er, enemy.

How was she supposed to feel about that? Why was it that you could hate someone so much one instant and then suddenly feel like you cared about them the next?

Stop thinking so much! the voice inside Madison's head bellowed. *Get back to work!*

Mr. Gibbons had moved along to the next topic. The students now read passages aloud from a short-story collection.

With the teacher distracted, Lindsay passed Madison a note.

Are you going to Egg's tomorrow? the note asked.

Madison scribbled back.

I guess so.

Madison flipped the note into the air, and it landed back on Lindsay's desk. Lindsay gave Madison a thumbs-up before burying her nose in her own book. Madison turned to her notebook—and her doodles—again.

Madison began writing on the newest journaling topic. It was a list.

Things I Have Lost
My favorite blue mittens in first grade
One of my backup disks with a month's worth of files!
My mom's aquamarine earrings that she loaned me for a birthday party at Aimee's
What else?
My mind?
Arrgggh.

Mrs. Gillespie came by the house on Saturday to pick Madison up. She had stayed with her dad after all, and gone home early the next morning.

Aimee didn't have dance class. "My teacher is sick again this week, and her replacement had a conflict," she explained sadly.

Fiona and Chet sat in the backseat. Mrs. Gillespie was making one more stop, to pick up Dan Ginsburg, another one of their good friends. It seemed to Madison that *everyone* was headed over to the Diaz house for the unveiling of Egg's new blog. Actually, the blog was really just a good excuse for everybody to hang out together. Señora Diaz, Egg's mother, had suggested that Egg invite a crowd over for do-it-yourself-tacos and games.

Madison was looking forward to seeing Hart, of course.

The weather hadn't improved much since the day before. It was still raining off and on. The wipers on the Gillespie car made a terrible squeak. Madison sat back in her seat and watched the rain beat against the windows. She was glad that her dad had let her spend the evening with Fiona instead of with him— and that her mom had allowed her to join everyone at Egg's house. Hanging with friends was putting Madison in a better mood even if it was raining out-side.

For some reason, Madison hadn't thought much about Ivy or Mrs. Daly since the previous day, but now that she sat in a car filled with her classmates, she began to worry again. She wondered what had kept Ivy out of school on Friday. The temptation was great to share what she'd learned with the rest of the group, but Madison kept her lips zipped. Mom had made Madison promise not to tell anyone, even the BFFs.

"I'm glad you're here," Madison told Aimee as they drove along. "Usually you're so busy on Saturdays with dance and all that."

"I'm glad you're here, too," Chet said from

the back of the car. "Or else we'd have no ride."

Everyone laughed, even Mrs. Gillespie.

"I just wish there was something I could do for my teacher," Aimee said. "It's hard seeing her sick like this."

Madison wondered how it felt for Ivy to watch her mom get sick. What would everyone in the car have said if *they* had known the truth about Ivy's situation? Would it make a difference in the way they treated Ivy?

Would it make a difference to Madison?

The car pulled up to Egg's house a little after noon.

"Welcome to my world," Egg said as he opened the door. He made a weird noise.

Fiona leaned over to Madison. "Walter's cute, and I like him a lot, but he can be really, *really* embarrassing sometimes," she admitted.

Madison smiled back at her. "He can be really embarrassing most of the time," she said with a loud laugh. "But don't forget, he's just being Egg."

Señora diaz strolled out of the kitchen wearing an apron with the words MI COMIDA ES EXCELENTE on it.

"*Buenos Días!*" Senora Diaz said. "How are you all doing?"

Almost everyone in the room had Señora Diaz as their Spanish teacher at FHJH, so stepping inside her home always felt a little awkward at first. She put everybody at their ease almost immediately, however. Gradually it began to feel like being around a friend—or at least a cool mom—and not a teacher who would grade you or quiz you. The room was packed with smiling faces that included those of Madison, Aimee, Fiona, Chet, and Dan. They moved into the kitchen to begin the tacos.

"Where's Hart?" Madison asked.

"Hart's on his way, with Drew," Egg said. "They had some family thing last night."

"Did you hear what happened to Ivy?" Dan asked.

"No, what?" Madison replied.

"I heard that she got her belly button pierced."

"I bet it looks hot," Chet said.

"Come on!" Aimee said.

"You have a one-track mind, Chet," Fiona grumbled.

The conversation was interrupted by the arrival of Hart and Drew. Everyone said their hellos. The topic of discussion stayed the same.

"I think Ivy is going to be kicked out of school," Aimee said. "What do you think?"

"I think that's an old rumor from, like, a million years ago," Madison said.

"Yes, but she's been absent. Does anyone know why?" Drew asked.

Madison almost blurted out, "I do!"

But she didn't.

Everyone piled the tomatoes and cheese and even the hot jalapeños onto their tacos. Madison poured on extra salsa. She loved Señora Diaz's homemade creations. When everyone was set, they moved in to the family room. They turned on the TV, and people spread out on the floor to eat.

Hart sat next to Madison. He gave her one of his jalapeños, and she thought her mouth had caught fire. But then he jumped right up and got Madison a glass of water, too. Madison could see Fiona across the room, sitting next to Egg, rolling her eyes at Madison as she always did.

The rain went *ping-ping-ping* on the roof of the Diaz house. Egg dragged everyone over to the computer to see his updated blog page for Disaster Zone, but just then, unfortunately, the computer froze. Then Drew took out a baseball-card collection that his grandfather had given to him recently. He always had something new to show off. He was one of the richest kids in Far Hills, and certainly in their crowd. His grandfather had Babe Ruth and Hank Aaron cards *and* an original Honus Wagner card, some of the most valuable ones available.

Conversation ebbed and flowed. The topics ranged from school (too much homework lately) to teachers (out of earshot of Señora Diaz, of course). Then somebody mentioned Ivy again, and Aimee laughed and repeated the gossip that they'd heard earlier that week, about the sophomore at Dunn Manor and Ivy's getting suspended.

Madison brooded.

She wanted to speak up and tell her friends that they had the wrong information, but she didn't.

How could she tell them the real deal when she didn't even know all the facts herself?

"It's working!" Egg yelled out as the Disaster Zone game screen finally reappeared. Everyone gathered around the computer to play.

"Who wants to team up?" Drew asked aloud.

Aimee grabbed Drew's arm. "I'm your partner," she declared. He nodded.

Chet and Fiona decided to pair up (instead of arguing, as they usually did). Egg and Dan were partners, too.

"That leaves Maddie and Hart," Aimee said with a smirk.

Hart smiled. "No prob," he said, reaching out to grab Madison's hand.

Madison thought she was going to faint when he did that. She would never have thought that she would enjoy playing Disaster Zone that much.

Chapter 10

Madison was feeling more and more like Harriet the Spy.

But it wasn't necessarily a good thing.

All week long she had been stealing glimpses of journal pages and listening to conversations from inside bathroom stalls. After all of her trying and prying, she'd learned some of the surprising truth about Ivy.

That was bad enough.

Now it was Sunday, and she was poking around online, looking for more and better clues to the truth about Bigwheels, too. It had been almost the entire weekend, and Madison's keypal still had not responded to Madison's pointed questions about Bloggerfishbowl.com.

Was Bigwheels avoiding Madison on purpose?

Finally, there was Mom—an entirely different mystery. Since Friday, Mom had worried aloud about what to wear for her big Sunday night meeting, and Madison couldn't help getting suspicious. Madison was certain that any "meeting" on a Sunday had to qualify as a date, especially when Mom's outfit was a main focus, and no matter how many times Mom insisted that the good impression she needed to make was for Budge Films.

"What should I wear?" Mom asked.

"What about that red dress you like so much? You haven't worn that in a long time," Madison said.

"The *red* one?" Mom laughed. "No, that would give the *wrong* impression, honey bear. I'd better stick to navy."

"But you look way prettier in the red one," Madison said with a little smile. "Wear it with your sparkly earrings. The diamond ones from Great-gramma Peg. They're good luck, aren't they?"

"Maddie, looking pretty isn't the goal here," Mom insisted. "This is serious work. And I need to look serious."

Madison wondered what kind of guy Mom must be seeing for dinner if she needed to look so serious. Was it a scientist? Or maybe an astronaut? Serious could be interesting. But serious could also be boring. What if the guy Mom was seeing was like Mr. Books? Not all librarians were boring, but he sure was.

In the midst of her dressing dilemma, Mom tossed Phin a treat. He danced around the room with delight. He hadn't eaten any dog snaps all day, and after each one he did a little twirl and let out his quiet, happy growl. Phineas T. Finn's stomach was a bottomless pit, at least when it came to Chow Bones, his favorite bacon-flavored snack.

Mom pulled on her nude hose and the navy dress with the buttons down the back. "Help me fasten these," she said to Madison.

Madison pinched the fabric together and fastened the buttons as Mom had directed. Each button was a different shade of pearl, and the row of them glistened all the way down Mom's back. In fact, everything about Mom, despite her "serious" pose, glistened a little bit just then. This was one of those moments when Madison saw just how beautiful her mother was.

"Will you be late tonight?" Madison asked as she did up the last button on the dress.

"Probably," Mom said. "You know how these things can go. I hope you don't mind staying with Dad and Stephanie—just in case I don't get back before your bedtime."

"Of course I don't mind," Madison said, even though she cringed at the notion of bedtime. Madison hadn't gone to bed much before eleven these past few months and she wasn't about to start now.

"I've seen a lot of Dad this week," Madison said. "I like seeing Dad. I mean, he *is* my dad. . . ."

"Oh, Maddie." Mom frowned. "I know I've been shuffling you off to your father's place all week. But it's all for a very good cause—believe me."

"Yeah?" Madison said, chewing on a hangnail.

"Yeah," Mom replied.

There was no good reason that Madison didn't come right out at that exact moment and ask Mom whom she was having dinner with—and why. But she didn't ask.

Then the doorbell rang.

"Good! Your father's here!" Mom gasped. "I have to go put on my shoes. Get the door, okay?"

Madison watched Mom trip over her stocking feet to get to her pair of navy high heels sitting in the hallway. In the meantime, Dad rang the bell twice more. Phin scratched and panted at the front door. Madison could hear Dad's voice loud and clear.

"Hold your horses, dog!" Dad chuckled. "I'm coming in."

Phin recognized Dad's voice and let out a howl.

"Rowororoorooooo!"

Reaching the door, Madison quickly unbolted it.

"Phinnie, get down!" Dad cried.

He shook his leg to stop Phin from jumping up on him, but the dog wrapped his paws around Dad's calf and wouldn't let go. Dad staggered to the side and kissed Madison hello. He grabbed a duffel bag sitting on the floor in the hall.

"Got everything you need for the night, laptop included?"

Madison nodded and smiled. Dad understood Madison's need to take her laptop everywhere. After all, he was the one who had first shown her how to use a computer. His business had him working on Web projects all the time. He always gave Madison little tips on scanning items for her files, downloading digital photos, and other miscellaneous computer tasks.

Mom's heels click-clacked on the floor as she appeared. "Jeffrey," Mom said with a toss of her head. Her voice was sweeter than usual. "Thanks again for coming to our rescue."

"Wow. You really do look great," Dad said, his eyes fixing on her ankles and then traveling all the way up. Madison saw him stare the way he had used to, but she knew it didn't really mean anything. No amount of wishing was going to reunite her parents. Madison had to keep telling herself that.

"Well, this is the big one," Mom told Dad. "I appreciate your support."

Dad extended his hand, and they shook but didn't kiss on the cheek. *That* might have meant something.

"Good luck, Francine," Dad said.

"Wait a minute. Are you guys speaking in code?"

Madison blurted out. "'Good luck'? 'This is the big one'? What are you two really talking about?"

"Big *meeting*, dear," Mom said.

"Good luck at the *meeting*," Dad said in reply.

Madison wasn't buying it. "Uh-huh," she sighed, "whatever you say." She hooked Phin's leash onto his collar and walked him through the door. Dad followed right behind.

"Bye," Madison said as she turned to blow Mom a kiss. "See you after school tomorrow?"

Mom winked. "You bet," she said, catching the kiss in the air.

During the car ride to her dad's apartment, Madison expected him to say something more about the way Mom was dressed or about the way he felt about her going on a big date. But strangely, he didn't say another word about Mom. Instead, he asked Madison about her journaling assignments.

Madison had shown both Dad and Stephanie the composition notebook on Thursday. She'd also mentioned Ivy's notebook—the one with the princess sticker. Dad knew Madison and Ivy's troubled history. He'd been around for first grade, when they had sworn to be friends forever—and for fourth grade, when they had declared they'd be enemies forever.

But Dad wasn't taking sides this time—at least, not Madison's side.

"This journal assignment is not a competition,

118

you know," Dad said. "Your journal entries are yours. And Ivy's are hers."

"What is that supposed to mean?" Madison asked defensively.

"Exactly what I said, Maddie. Some things are meant to be private. . . ." Dad said. "Some secrets are not meant to be shared—until the person is ready to share them."

"That's exactly what Mom said," Madison groaned.

"Well, she's right."

"I told you, Dad, I didn't mean to look at Ivy's journal. I just . . . peeked."

"Well, then you should just forget what you saw. Ivy's entitled to her 'perfect life,' Maddie, no matter how much you may dislike her for it," Dad said.

"How can she be entitled to a perfect life when it's not even perfect?" Madison asked. "No one's life is perfect. She's a total liar!"

"Look, Maddie," Dad said, a little more sternly this time. "Is everything you write in your journal the whole truth and nothing but the truth? Don't you ever write dreams or wishes? And don't you think Ivy is allowed to do the same?"

Madison didn't like being lectured, especially not on a subject like that. After all, Ivy was the enemy, right? And journals were *Madison's* domain. She was the writer. She made the collages. She was the one who used bigfishbowl.com more than anyone.

"Writing in journals online or off is a very personal matter," Dad continued. "We've talked about this before. I thought you understood. You wouldn't want Ivy to take just a 'quick peek' at your words, would you?"

Dad had his eyes on the road, so he didn't see Madison make a face. Nor did he hear her make a "hmmmph" sound, as if she were super annoyed at what he'd said. She pressed her cheek firmly against the window on the passenger's side—a vain attempt at getting as far away from Dad as possible. Of course, "getting away" in a car was an impossible feat. All she could do was squish herself up against the door while her cheek got extra cold from the glass.

Dad pulled the car into the garage of his apartment building and parked alongside a large white Hummer.

"What a waste of space," Dad mumbled when he saw the huge car. "Those things shouldn't be allowed on the road."

Madison wasn't listening. She was too busy staying mad about their earlier conversation. As they exited the car, she had a single-minded plan: to go online. She needed to write down some of the feelings that were swirling around inside her head.

Stephanie wasn't at the apartment when Madison got there, so Madison went directly into the room reserved for her at Dad's and booted up the laptop.

The e-mailbox was blinking.

FROM   SUBJECT
✉ GoGramma   Winter Scarf
✉ GoGramma   Winter Scarf
✉ Wetwinz   Re: My Teacher
✉ Bigwheels   JSS
✉ BalletGrl   My Teacher

Gramma Helen had sent the same e-mail twice. She did that sometimes. Once, she'd sent Madison seven copies of the same e-mail.

Today she wanted to know what colors Madison was wearing. Every winter, Gramma knitted a scarf for her granddaughter—and she wanted to make sure that it matched whatever was in Madison's closet.

After the double e-mail from GoGramma, Madison opened the message from Fiona—a response to an e-mail that Aimee had forwarded to both of them, and to Lindsay, earlier that afternoon.

From: Wetwinz
To: BalletGrl; MadFinn; LINDSAY
Subject: Re: My Teacher
Date: Sun 17 Oct 4:12 PM
───────────────────────────────
OMG Aim I am sososoSO sorry about
your teacher. And I'm sorry 2 b/c
we're having guests for dinner and
Mom says I can't go out. Maybe we
can all go and visit ur teacher

this week? Let me know. I'm
thinking of you.
xoxo

Fiona

p.s.: Will u be walking 2 school
tomorrow? Chet's getting sick and
Maddie I know ur @ yr dad's right?
LYLAs!

--Original Message--
From: BalletGrl
To: MadFinn; Wetwinz; LINDSAY
Subject: My Teacher
Date: Sun 17 Oct 2:46 PM

I have incredibly bad news and
that is my dance teacher is in the
hospital again. I guess she had a
side effect or something I'm not
sure. N e way I'm going to make her
a card today and I was wondering if
u guys would come over 18r to help
me make it. My brothers are being
so annoying to me. They just don't
understand what I feel like to know
someone so close to me who is sick
like this. I don't know if I will
ever be able to dance the same again.

:*;

Aim

Madison hit REPLY.

```
From: MadFinn
To: BalletGrl; Wetwinz; LINDSAY
Subject: Re: My Teacher
Date: Sun 17 Oct 5:38 PM
```
Wow that is bad news Aim. But I'm @
Dad's place and can't come over.
Maybe we should talk tonight? I feel
so bad. I wish there was
someone u could talk 2 who
understood what u felt

Madison paused before finishing her sentence. Of course there *was* someone Aimee could talk to—Ivy. If Aimee only knew! Madison typed up something else for the end of her e-mail and hit SEND. Then she opened the one remaining unopened e-mail, from her keypal.

At last.

```
From: Bigwheels
To: MadFinn
Subject: JSS
Date: Sun 17 Oct 4:59 PM
```
JSS 4 everything. I know u wanted
me to talk about the whole blog
thing this week and I wasn't really
up for talking. I don't want u 2 be
mad or upset or left out. I WANT to

keep it real with you. I do. That's why I'm writing now.

The thing is--the reason I was writing about all that on the blog--well, it's because we found out that my brother has been diagnosed with mild autism. My parents have known for a while but they weren't talking about it that much. And I know "mild" makes it seem like it's not so bad, but it's hard to be around him sometimes--SO hard.

I know I'm not the only person on earth who has a brother with autism, but I feel like I am sometimes. Most people stare when my brother acts all weird in public and I want to scream at them. He hits himself sometimes. I love him but he embarrasses me, you know? He never sits still and he hates it when I touch him.

So that was what I was not talking about. I just froze up at the thought of telling u. I've written and rewritten this e-mail to you about ten times this weekend b/c I wanted it 2 be perfect. Of course u of all ppl should know the truth.

```
Thanks for listening/reading. I'll
write more 18r.

Yours till the ear waxes (LOL),

Vicki aka Bigwheels
```

Madison read all the way to the end and then went back up to the top. Was she reading this correctly? *Bigwheels had a brother with autism?*

All at once the air around Madison felt heavier than heavy, closing in on her like a wool blanket, choking her. It was hard to breathe.

Wait. Life wasn't supposed to be this serious—was it?

Madison opened her files.

 `Keep It Real (continued)`

Madison paused and read the file name aloud. Then she read it again.

She wanted to type, but the words wouldn't come. Her fingers remained suspended above the keyboard in a state of paralysis.

All she could do was stare at the cursor.
Blink, blink, blink.

What was Madison supposed to do with this new, difficult information—about Ivy, about Bigwheels? Was it possible that sometimes even *Madison* didn't know how to keep it real?

Chapter 11

Mr. Danehy seemed to be feeling a hundred percent better on Monday.

Actually, it was more like a hundred and ten percent. No more congestion, loud coughing, or spraying sneezes. He was like Tigger bouncing around in front of the blackboard at the front of the room.

"Boys and girls, I have your quizzes from the library the other day," Mr. Danehy announced with a lilt in his voice. Every move he made was way out of character for him. Madison half expected him to do a backflip. Was it his cold medicine?

Normally when Mr. Danehy passed out tests that he'd graded, he would make a little speech about how everyone could have tried harder or studied longer or done something more, more, MORE. Then he would announce, in a low, serious, and very grouchy voice, that he had decided to grade on a wide curve, "because the grades were just that bad."

However, today the only curve in Mr. Danehy's classroom was his ear-to-ear grin.

"You'll be happy to know, students, that I gave everyone an A," he said as he walked around the room and dropped the tests on the desks.

Madison's jaw dropped. *Everyone* had gotten an A? Ivy had gotten an A?!!

"I am so-o-o glad I didn't waste time studying," Ivy said under her breath. "Because it didn't even matter in the end, did it? So there."

This turn of events made Madison queasy. She didn't have a head cold, but her head was stuffed nonetheless—with thoughts of Bigwheels's brother, Aimee's teacher, Ivy's mother, and more.

Madison turned to Poison Ivy.

"Um . . . where were you on Friday?" Madison asked.

"Busy," Ivy snapped. "Why?"

"Just wondering," Madison said, drumming her fingers on the lab table. "Um . . . because . . ."

Grrrrrr.

Why couldn't Madison come up with a good follow-up question?

Ivy was unfazed by the entire exchange. She sat

up tall in her seat and waited for Madison to talk. But when Madison didn't come through with the compelling next question, Ivy let out an enormous, annoyed sigh.

Madison watched as Ivy leaned over and wrote a note, probably to Rose Thorn. Normally the enemy was a text-messaging kind of girl, but that wasn't allowed in classes, not even on Ivy's perfect pink cell phone. Madison was tempted, but she restrained herself from reading Ivy's paper note. Glancing at things had gotten her into enough trouble that week.

After folding the note, Ivy checked her face in her compact, puckering up to add a smear of lip gloss that smelled like raspberries.

Up at the front of the classroom, Mr. Danehy wrote a long list of biology vocabulary words on the board. He asked the class to copy down the list and look up the definitions in the backs of their science textbooks.

Madison could barely concentrate. She was distracted by the smell of Ivy's lip gloss, the chattering of the boys in the next row, the scraping of the chalk on the board, and the squeak of Mr. Danehy's ugly black shoes.

How could someone whose mom was so sick be acting so . . . indifferent? Madison knew that if she had been in Ivy's platform shoes, she'd be crying or throwing up or something just as stressed out.

Just the idea of seeing her own mom get sick with something as serious as breast cancer made Madison swoon. It was the worst possible thought in a sea of impossible thoughts.

Madison wanted to turn to Ivy and ask her what was *really* going on. Forget old wounds. Forget being sworn enemies. This was more real than all of that. Wasn't it?

"Ivy, I wanted to . . ." Madison started to speak, but her voice faded away.

"Hey! Guess what happened to me yesterday?" Ivy said.

Madison's eyes lit up when she realized that this might be the moment when all would be revealed. Her eyes met Ivy's.

"*What* happened to you yesterday?" Madison asked cautiously.

"Well . . . I got a ticket to see Jimmy J and a bunch of other bands," Ivy bragged. "The Wallapawooza concert. It's in two weeks."

Madison made a face. "Wallapa-what?"

Ivy sneered, "Wallapawooza. Hello? It's only, like, the best concert around. I heard they were sold out in under a half hour, or maybe less."

"Gee," Madison said. She waited a moment longer, to see if Ivy had anything more to say.

"I bet you wish *you* had tickets to Wallapawooza," Ivy said.

"Sure," Madison shrugged. "Whatever you say."

Madison glanced up and saw Hart looking over from across the room. He crossed his eyes and stuck out his tongue. Madison knew he was directing that face at Ivy. She let out a little giggle.

"Who are you laughing at?" Ivy snapped.

"You," Madison said, giggling a little more.

"Come on, you're just jealous because I go to cool concerts and you don't," Ivy said with a snarl.

Madison sat there without responding, because, of course, she was not jealous. Right now she was worried.

"I know that you wish you had a life like mine," Ivy went on. "And did I tell you that I get to meet the bands after the concert, too?"

"Oh?" Madison asked.

"Sure. My mom made all the arrangements. She's been working with this really important concert pro-moter lately, and they made this deal that she can get the best tickets to all the best concerts. Isn't that cool?"

"Cooler than cool," Madison mumbled. She gazed up into Ivy's eyes to see if her enemy would blink—and let the truth slip. Madison knew Ivy's mom hadn't really set that up. But Ivy didn't blink once. She kept piling on the lies.

"My mom is so-o-o-o connected," Ivy bragged.

"How is your mom?" Madison asked.

"What do you care?"

"I don't know. I just haven't seen her since you

had that school party at your house a while ago and . . ."

"Since when do you care about my mother?" Ivy snapped.

Madison backed off. "It was just a question," she said.

"Quit acting jealous," Ivy said again. "You are so predictable."

That night at home, Madison sat at the kitchen table as Mom flew around her, waving spatulas and forks and wooden spoons. Mom was whistling (and Mom hardly ever whistled). She wasn't wearing any shoes (and Mom always wore shoes).

Was Madison in the right kitchen?

"I decided to cook us a big dinner tonight," Mom said. "A really big celebratory dinner of linguini with sun-dried tomatoes and yellow peppers and . . ."

"Mom, what's all this about?" Madison asked.

"I'm feeling good tonight," Mom answered. "No, I take that back. I'm feeling fantastic!"

"You mean after your date?" Madison asked.

"Date?" Mom said. "What date?"

"Last night's date," Madison said. "The one you shipped me off to Dad's house for."

"Shipped you off?" Mom burst into laughter. "I thought you said you didn't mind staying over with Dad and Stephanie."

"I just mind the fact that you're dating some

131

guy *seriously*, and you haven't even told me about it yet."

"Madison Francesca Finn, what on earth are you talking about? I was *not* on a date last night. I told you that a dozen times. Your dad told you, too."

"Yeah, but you were just saying that so I wouldn't feel bad. Why else would you have gotten all dressed up in your best clothes and your expensive shoes? Why else would you want me out of the house?"

"Oh, no!" Mom interrupted Madison's train of thought. "Aw, honey bear. You have the wrong idea."

Madison crossed her arms in front of her and looked away.

"Maddie," Mom continued, "look at me. Please."

Madison turned back to Mom.

"If I were dating someone," Mom said, "don't you think I would tell you?"

"Maybe."

"No, definitely," Mom said, squeezing Madison's shoulder. "I would never keep something that important from you. *Never.*"

"You wouldn't?" Madison asked.

Mom shook her head. "I promise you."

Madison took a deep breath—a deep breath of relief—and wrapped her arms around Mom's shoulders.

"So why were you so nervous about what to

wear? Why did I have to go over to Dad's place? What was going on?"

A huge smile spread across Mom's face.

"What is it? What?" Madison asked. Her curiosity was piqued.

"I got a promotion," Mom said. "A big one."

"You did?"

"Well, it's not final, but I'm pretty sure that I'll be named executive producer at Budge Films. I had my last meeting with the head of the company on Sunday. And last week, I had to pull together some portfolio materials for another last-minute meeting. I didn't want to tell you until I knew it was a sure thing."

Madison jumped into the air. "So you're not dating an astronaut?"

"No," Mom said with a chuckle. "I'm not. But I might make a movie about one someday."

They both laughed.

"You don't have to worry about my dating anyone, honey bear," Mom said. "It's just you and me and Phinnie—at least for the time being."

"Why didn't you tell me what was *really* going on?" Madison sniffled.

"I don't know, Maddie. I probably should have told you sooner. I just really wanted it to be the right time. I'm sorry," Mom replied.

"How did Dad know?"

"Well," Mom said slowly. "I told him."

"Huh? You told Dad and not me?" Madison flung herself onto a chair in the living room.

"Oh, it shouldn't matter that I told your father . . ."

"But it does matter," Madison said.

"Maddie, don't be mad. . . ."

"I can't believe you told Dad and not me. . . ."

"Maddie, please listen. I love you. This is *good* news—my promotion. It means good things for all of us," Mom said.

"Yeah, but you didn't tell me first," Madison said again.

Without another word to Mom, she got up, walked out of the room, and went upstairs. Phin trotted behind her. Mom didn't stop either of them. She'd obviously decided to let Madison have some time alone.

Lying on top of her butterfly-patterned coverlet, Madison spied her laptop sitting open in the exact same spot where she'd left it that morning. But Madison felt like writing in her composition book instead of typing on the laptop.

She reached for her favorite orange pencil. Although she still hadn't finished her weekend assignment, she already had another question to tackle.

Journaling #7
Topic: Did you ever run away from home? How far did you get?

134

Madison laughed to herself. She *always* felt like running away. It was as if Mr. Gibbons had written that question just for her. In a way, she had just run away from Mom.

There was a time, long ago, when Phin had run away from home, too. The pug had gotten a few blocks away on half-frozen paws. He had been chasing something—a cat, a bird, or some other creature—and had lost his way. But that didn't count. Madison needed to talk about a time when *she* had run away.

She stared down at the blank journal page. All at once, her pencil started moving, but she wasn't writing. She was scribbling flowers and lightning bolts and three-dimensional cubes. Madison wrote her name a few times, too, in capital block letters with stripes and dots in the middle.

She was making pretty pictures, for sure. But Madison wasn't answering Mr. Gibbons's question. Not even close.

Journals, blogs, e-mails—Madison needed time and inspiration to write things that really mattered. But for the second day in a row, Madison had nothing to write, nothing to say.

Nothing.

She couldn't be all out of words, could she?

Not when there were so many things that still needed explaining.

Chapter 12

"Did you see what Ivy was wearing today?" Lindsay blurted out at the lunch table on Tuesday.

Aimee nodded. "She is looking terrible these days. I think we should alert the fashion police."

Lindsay made a whirring noise like a speeding ambulance.

All the girls cracked up.

"What if she's doing drugs with that Dunn Manor guy?" Fiona suggested.

Madison shot Fiona a look. "No way," Madison said. "Drugs? Come on. I know she's bad, but she's not into that."

"It could happen," Aimee said. "My brother Doug said that the guy Ivy was dating at Dunn was suspended this week for bad behavior. Maybe Ivy's been spending too much time at his place. It's like an after-school special gone wild. . . ."

Lindsay started giggling uncontrollably.

"Yeah? Can you imagine if Ivy got suspended? It would be like an FHJH national disaster," Fiona said.

"What would the drones do without their fearless leader?" Aimee said.

"I'd love to see the look on Rose and Joanie's faces," Lindsay said.

"Maybe Ivy is just tired," Madison said. "She has bad weeks, too."

"Are you defending her?" Aimee asked.

Madison held her hands up in a pose of surrender. "No, no!" she insisted. "But I just think . . . that maybe . . . we're being a little harsh. . . ."

Lindsay, Aimee, and Fiona burst into laughter.

"What is so funny?" Madison asked.

"Maddie, we're talking about the Queen of Harsh here, Poison Ivy Daly, remember? How could we possibly come near her level of mean?" Aimee asked.

Madison nodded. "You're right. I know."

She was beginning to feel a little self-conscious in front of her BFFs. The last thing she wanted her friends to know was that she felt sorry for the enemy. Then again, they might feel sympathetic, too, if they had only known the whole truth. If they had known that Ivy's mom was suffering from

137

cancer, they might have had second thoughts about the way they were behaving.

As the girls sat there thinking of more names to call Ivy, Egg and Drew strolled up to the orange table at the back of the cafeteria and sat down on some benches nearby. Their arms were loaded with binders and books. Egg looked mad.

"Maddie!" Egg growled. "What are you doing sitting here?"

"Having lunch," Madison said.

"Haven't you forgotten something?" Egg asked.

Madison blinked twice. She had no idea what Egg was talking about. But then she remembered. They were supposed to have met up in Mrs. Wing's classroom during lunch to work on the school Web pages.

"Oops," Madison said.

She picked up her tray with its unfinished ham-and-cheese sandwich, unopened bag of chips, and carton of chocolate milk. After saying good-bye to her girlfriends, she followed Egg and Drew up to the computer lab.

Mrs. Wing was waiting. She'd pulled up the home-page screen. Madison, Egg, Drew, and Lance's mouths fell open.

"That is so *amazing*!" Drew said.

"You reformatted the entire site?" Madison asked in disbelief.

"In only a week?" Lance said.

Mrs. Wing stood back and tipped her head to the side. "I've been promising Principal Bernard for weeks that I would get this done," she said. "And now I finally have done it. Surprise!"

"This is tripping me out," Egg said. "It's not like some boring school Web pages. Wow."

On the screen was a full-sized photo of the exterior of FHJH. In the corner of the photo, at the top of the actual flagpole, Mrs. Wing had added an animated blue-and-white flag (the FHJH school colors, naturally). It said, ENTER HERE.

When Egg clicked on the flag, the screen dissolved in a flash of blue and white. Then a menu appeared.

"This is fantastic," Madison said.

A scrolling marquee went across the top of the page underneath the name Far Hills Junior High, printed in bold, blue letters. And underneath that, Mrs. Wing had created a menu of hypertext links for each page on the site: Sports and Extracurricular Activities; Teacher Resources; Homework Café; and more.

After a tour of the site's many pages, Madison and her friends were feeling quite overwhelmed. But they were also excited by the challenge. Working on the site would be more fun than ever before.

Mrs. Wing was happier than happy, too. "I think our recent journaling project in the seventh grade has gotten you students more interested in writing," she said. "I'm thinking about adding a bulletin board on our site—and having links, for all of the teachers to post homework assignments. What do you think?"

"More homework?" Lance groaned.

Madison laughed. "Lance," she said, "what Mrs. Wing means is that teachers can post homework online in addition to giving us work sheets or whatever."

"Welcome to the twenty-first century, Far Hills Junior High," Egg said.

Mrs. Wing chuckled.

Of course, the very best part of the site redo was the fact that it helped Madison to forget, however briefly, the events of the past few days. For an hour or so, she completely forgot Ivy, Bigwheels, and even Mom.

Then, with her head feeling unfuzzy for the first time in days, Madison exited Mrs. Wing's classroom and breezed through the rest of her classes. At three o'clock she met up with Fiona and Aimee by the lockers. Fiona's soccer practice had been canceled. Aimee had finished a last-period makeup science test.

Outside, the sky was one enormous gray cloud that followed the trio all the way home. Was rain coming again?

"That was hands down the easiest science test I've ever taken," Aimee bragged. "I think Mrs.

Wayne makes the questions easier now because she can't deal with grading hard tests. She's older than my grandmother."

"Sometimes she just stops in the middle of a thought, and I think it's because she forgot what she wanted to say," Fiona added. "It's funny."

"I bet you wish you had our science section instead of yours with Mr. Danehy, right, Maddie?" Aimee said.

Madison nodded. "Yeah. Science class without Mr. Danehy and without Poison Ivy. I wish."

"Speaking of Ivy . . ." Aimee said, "did anyone see her this afternoon?"

"Why?" Madison sighed. She couldn't believe that Fiona and Aimee wanted to continue the Ivy gossip from lunch.

"No biggie," Aimee said. "I just saw her *crying* outside one of the bathrooms. Can you believe it? Ivy never cries. She's more like an emotional freezer. She doesn't care about anyone else except herself."

Madison felt a twinge inside her chest.

"What was she crying about?" Fiona asked.

"Herself," Aimee joked. "She ran out of lip gloss. Oooh! Poor me!"

Fiona laughed.

Madison felt another twinge inside. She wasn't laughing. This wasn't funny . . . at all.

"Look at me, I'm Ivy," Aimee said, prancing away, flipping her hair and then stopping on the street to pose. "Do you like my new outfit? It only cost ten million dollars, and I have it in eleven different colors, including leather. Oooh!"

Fiona was normally the one who refrained from bad-mouthing anyone, especially people at school. This time, however, she couldn't stop laughing. And so it was up to Madison to say something . . . nice.

"I think Ivy's got a problem," Madison started to say.

"*No kidding!*" Aimee yelled.

Fiona laughed harder.

"No, you two, I'm serious. I think maybe she has a real problem," Madison said.

Aimee and Fiona stopped laughing.

"You're serious," Fiona said.

"Like, what problem?" Aimee said. "What do you know that you aren't telling us?"

"I just . . ." Madison remembered her promise to keep Mrs. Daly's condition a secret. "I don't know anything for sure. But I just think that maybe Ivy is really sad. Maybe she's not being a drama queen for once."

"I guess you could be right," Fiona said hesitantly.

"Come on!" Aimee cried. "Please! I can't stay for this pity party."

Madison cracked a little smile. "I didn't mean to be *so* serious. . . ."

"Then don't be!" Aimee said.

"Hey, I know her!" Fiona said, pointing across the

142

street. She raised her arm and waved. "Hello, Mrs. Reynolds! How's Pete?" she called out.

The woman smiled and waved back.

"Who is that?" Aimee asked as the woman walked away.

"Oh, she's just this lady. My mom tutors her kid, Pete. He's three, and he has autism," Fiona explained.

Madison stopped short. "Did you say 'autism'?"

"Sometimes he can't stand being touched. And he flaps his arms like a bird," Fiona explained. "But Mrs. Reynolds is the most incredible mother."

"What is autism?" Aimee asked.

Madison started to answer but she bit her tongue. The truth was that after reading Bigwheels's blog, she'd already researched the complete definition of autism and all of its symptoms online. But she didn't want to sound like a know-it-all, so she let Fiona do the talking.

Fiona thought for a moment. "Autism has something to do with your brain. Sometimes kids don't talk right away, that kind of thing. At least that's what my mom tells me," she said. "Of course, I know it's more complicated than that."

"Gee, I'm impressed," Aimee said.

"Well, I only know a little," Fiona said.

"It's so weird that you saw Mrs. Reynolds like that, because I was just wondering about autism," Madison said.

"Huh? You were?" Aimee said. "Maddie, why were you wondering about *that*?"

Madison gulped.

"Oh, I don't know, Aim, I saw a TV show on autism once . . . and I—I've just always wondered about it. That's all."

"That's so random, Maddie," Aimee said.

"You should ask my mother if you want to know more," Fiona suggested. "I'm sure she could answer any questions you have."

"Er . . . thanks," Madison mumbled, wanting to change the subject. For some reason she didn't feel like telling Aimee or Fiona about Bigwheels and Eddie. But it did get her thinking. If Fiona knew someone who had it, maybe autism wasn't so strange or scary.

"Did you do the latest journaling assignment?" Aimee asked her friends.

"I'm still working on the last two," Madison admitted with a groan.

"I like the latest question that Mrs. Quill gave us," Fiona said. She repeated it: "Pretend to look at the world from someone else's point of view."

"I pretended to be a prima ballerina," Aimee said with a twirl.

"Oh, that's a great one. Maybe I'll write as Mia Hamm, soccer champion," Fiona said.

"What about you, Maddie? Did Mr. Gibbons give you the same question?" Aimee asked.

"Yeah, he did. But I don't know what to write," Madison said.

They reached the bend in the road, where Fiona turned off Blueberry Street to get to her house. At the last minute, Aimee decided to veer off with her. She'd left something over at the Waterses' house the last time she had visited.

"E us later!" Fiona and Aimee called out to Madison at the exact same time.

"E me, too!" Madison giggled, waving them on.

When she arrived home, Madison walked heavily up her porch steps, thinking hard. The door was unlocked, but Mom was nowhere to be found.

"Hello?" Madison called out. She could hear radio static coming from the kitchen. "Is anyone here?"

Madison noticed that the dog's leash wasn't hanging on its hook, which was a huge relief. That meant Mom and Phin were probably taking a walk around the block—or maybe even all the way to the park. Mom liked to escape with the dog sometimes when she'd been at her computer all day. At the dog run in the park, Phin could hang out with the other dogs, and Mom could hang out with the other moms (and dads and grandmothers and kids). It was a nice break for them both.

With the house all to herself, Madison threw down her jacket, kicked off her sneakers, and curled up in one corner of the downstairs sofa.

After the walk home from school, Madison finally felt a kernel of inspiration ready to pop.

She booted up her computer, opened her e-mail box, and hit NEW.

From: MadFinn
To: Bigwheels
Subject: Re: JSS
Date: Tues 19 Oct 3:33 PM
_____
OK so I owe u an apology. I'm JSS2!!!

I know I asked u all those important questions about ur blog and then you answered me with all the details BUT then how lame am I b/c I didn't write back??? I have no reason or excuse, I just didn't. But I was thinking about all the things u said. I was thinking a lot. 4 1 thing, ur amazing, Vicki. Not only do u always give me good advice, but I feel like u think about things that really matter and u know how 2 talk about them.

When u finally told me about Eddie I was blown away. Well, if I'm being really honest--at first I was REALLY mad b/c u didn't tell me sooner. (I wish u could have

trusted me.) But then I stopped
feeling upset b/c I thought about
the whole situation from your point
of view. I can't imagine what it's
like not being able to hug him. It
must be sad. I don't have a brother
but I would lose my mind if I
couldn't hug Phinnie.

Pleez know that I'm here if u need
2 talk about it n e other time. OK?

Yours till the friend ships,

Maddie

p.s.: Are there n e other secrets u
feel like sharing?

Chapter 13

Mom was in the mood to buy shoes. She'd been in the mood to shop ever since her executive producer promotion had come through. And so, after school on Wednesday, she and Madison headed over to the Far Hills Shoppes together.

Madison and Mom raced around the shops on the mezzanine level and then boarded the escalator to the first floor. Although Madison had been feeling tired during the last class at school, she felt energized by being at the mall. Was it the steady flow of people moving in and out of stores? Or maybe the music piped in through the loudspeakers? Or was it a combination of flashing neon lights and the loud *brrrring* of cash registers?

It was all of those things *and* the sales—with all those exclamation points!

Hurry! 20% Off Entire Inventory!
Buy two pairs—get one free!
Don't miss it! Huge closeout sale! One day only!

After shopping for only an hour, Madison and Mom had purchased not one, but three pairs of shoes (including one free pair), a pair of dangling, purple-beaded earrings (Mom had convinced Madison to try them on), and a silk scarf that Mom was sure would look just right at her first official board meeting as a Budge Films executive producer.

"This is actually fun," Madison said to Mom as they headed into yet another shoe store. "But do we really need anything else, Mom? You're a little out of control." Her mom just smiled and nodded.

Madison liked being at the mall, but she wasn't always into buying stuff. Aimee never understood that. How could a person like to shop—and not actually *shop*? But Madison always said that it was because shopping was a group activity. She liked to shop because it meant hanging out with whomever she was with: Aimee, Fiona, or, as today, Mom.

"Wow. I haven't let myself do this in a long time," Mom said aloud. She giggled. "I love it. I love being here with you."

"I'm sorry again about yesterday," Madison said.

Mom squeezed Madison's arm. "Me, too. But we covered that ground already. Let's just shop! Woohoo!"

Madison laughed at the image of her mom as Super Shopper. What was that manic look in Mom's eyes? Craziness? Or was it just happiness? Usually Mom seemed so consumed by work that she hardly ever stopped to have a good time. This week, however, Madison had seen another side to Mom.

She liked it.

"Francine?" a woman's voice said near the lingerie store, where they'd stopped to look in the window.

"Huh?" Mom turned to face the person who'd called her name. "Paige?"

Madison turned, too. Standing there in the middle of the mall were Mrs. Daly and her daughter, Poison Ivy.

"Paige! What are you doing here?" Mom asked Mrs. Daly.

"Oh, I thought it would be nice to come out and shop a bit," Mrs. Daly replied. "I've been a little cooped up lately, as you know. My doctor says I need the air." She reached for Ivy's arm. "And I get to spend some time with Ivy, too," Mrs. Daly said with a smile.

Ivy smiled, too. Madison tried to decide whether it was one of her typical, forced smiles or not.

"Hello, Ivy," Madison said.

"Hey," Ivy said.

Something about Ivy's face looked sad—very different from the raspberry-lip-gloss look she had at school.

"I just lo-o-o-ve that sweater!" Mrs. Daly gushed, reaching over to tug Madison's sleeve. "That color looks great on you, Maddie. And you look great, too! We don't see enough of you these days."

Mom put her hands on Madison shoulders. "Yes, Paige. She's all grown up. So is Ivy! How's that for fast? Where did the years go?"

The two mothers laughed.

Madison and Ivy did not laugh.

Madison squirmed. If she had had to write the script of the best mall trip ever, transformed into the worst mall trip ever, it would star one person and one person only: Ivy Renee Daly.

Of course, after only a few minutes Mom and Mrs. Daly started chatting more intently. They were practically standing on each other's toes.

Meanwhile, Madison and Ivy were left standing by themselves, and they weren't talking.

"So, you were shopping?" Madison finally asked. Someone needed to break the ice.

Ivy flipped her red hair. "Yes, we were shopping. Were you?"

"Yes," Madison said. "Did you buy anything?"

"Yes," Ivy said. "Did you?"

"Yes," Madison answered.

151

As accompaniment to their dull conversation, mall music played in the background. A too-loud instrumental version of "Monster Mash" blared out of speakers directly over their heads. Madison guessed it was in honor of the Halloween season.

"Nice song, right?" Madison joked.

"Yeah, right," Ivy said sarcastically.

"So . . ." Madison said.

"So . . ." Ivy said.

"Did you do the journaling assignment yet?" Madison had to ask something real, and that seemed as good a question as any.

Ivy shrugged. "I haven't written much since last week."

Madison frowned. That was an awfully honest answer from the enemy. It took her by surprise. She wanted to say, "Gee, Ivy, what happened to your perfectly perfect life, huh? Huh? *Huh*?"

But she didn't.

They stood there quietly for a moment. The moms were still having a major powwow. Madison's mom actually put her arm around Mrs. Daly at one point.

Ivy finally spoke up.

"Well," Ivy said. "I guess you know."

"Know?" Madison said. "What?"

"Oh, come on," Ivy said. "You know."

Madison looked down at the floor. "Okay. I know."

"Huge bummer, right?" Ivy said.

152

Madison wasn't totally sure they were talking about the same thing.

"Bummer? You mean your mom being sick?"

Ivy looked away. "Yeah," she said softly. "It's a bummer. Nothing is the same anymore."

Madison thought that there were probably a million words to describe someone's mom being sick, but "bummer" wasn't one of the first ones she would have picked. But how could she fault Ivy for her choice of words? Ivy's mother *was* sick—really sick. There was a teeny part of Madison that wanted to put her arm around Ivy, just as her mom had put her arm around Ivy's mom.

"So I guess that's why I haven't been able to write a lot in that dumb journal," Ivy continued.

"Yeah," Madison said, trying to sound sympathetic. "I guess."

"Look, please don't say anything."

"About what?" Madison asked.

"About my mother," Ivy said. "I really don't want anyone to know. I don't want them to know she lost all her hair, and I don't want everyone treating me like I'm a leper because I have a sick mother."

"What are you talking about?"

"Just don't tell," Ivy said. "Or else. I mean it."

Madison's eyes opened wide. "Fine. I won't say a word."

"You'd better not," Ivy said sharply. "If I find out that you do . . ."

All of a sudden, the two mothers burst into laughter. Mrs. Daly's eyes were tearing, and she seemed out of breath.

"Are you okay, Mom?" Ivy asked. Her expression shifted from menacing scowl to a look of genuine concern and love.

Mrs. Daly shook her head. "Oh . . . Ivy . . . I'm fine . . . just something . . . funny Mrs. Finn said. . . ."

Ivy pursed her lips. "Oh. Okay."

Madison stared at Ivy's face. In an instant the enemy's whole demeanor changed. In an instant she stopped being the person who had been giving Madison such a hard time a few moments before— and in school all week. In fact, right now Ivy looked afraid. Or was it sad? Ivy's eyes appeared misty, too, although she would never have admitted that she was close to tears. Not in the mall—and certainly not in the presence of her number one enemy, Madison.

"We'd better be going," Mom said.

Mrs. Daly leaned over and kissed Mom's cheek. "Congratulations again, Frannie. I am so glad we keep bumping into each other."

"Let's really do that lunch date," Mom said.

Mrs. Daly nodded. "Definitely."

"Okay, girls," Mom said, giving Madison a little nudge and smiling at Ivy. "There's more shopping to be done!"

Ivy and Madison exchanged another glance, and their eyes locked, just for a moment. Were they sharing something? Another secret? Somewhere, deep down, despite all the bluster and the anger and the rude remarks, did they understand each other better than anyone could ever know?

"See you in school," Madison said.

"Yeah," Ivy said.

"Good luck on your journaling assignment," Madison said.

"Yeah, I'm sure it'll be perfect," Ivy said.

Madison gave Ivy a tiny smile. "Perfect," she said.

Mrs. Daly gave Madison a peck on the cheek. "You are such a beautiful girl!" she said, throwing her arms around Madison for a hug.

Madison didn't understand why Ivy's mom was being so affectionate. But she let her be that way. It seemed to make her happy. Madison hugged her back.

"Okay, okay," Mom said. "Let's stop our long good-bye. I'll call you, Paige. Good-bye, Ivy."

"Good-bye, Mrs. Finn," Ivy said.

"So long!" Mrs. Daly said.

As they walked away, Mom turned to Madison. "Ivy's mother looks pretty good, don't you think?"

"Yeah, she does," Madison said. "At least, I think so."

"Well, she just got some bad news," Mom said. "She needs to go in for even more treatment. They're waiting until the new year, though. It's just a lot to handle. Apparently Ivy's older sister, Janet,

155

may take some time off from school. Oh, Maddie, I am so glad we're all healthy. We are very lucky."

"I know," Madison said.

"What did you girls talk about? I know you and Ivy don't exactly get along. . . ." Mom said.

"We talked about school and science class. She told me about her mom—a little bit. Not much."

"Well, I'm glad to see that you two can be civil in a public place," Mom joked.

"Yeah," Madison said, distracted. She glanced across the mall in time to see Ivy and her mother reach the escalator. She watched as they stepped on and disappeared to the floor below.

Just before they vanished from view, Ivy turned.

Madison didn't know if she was looking back at her or just looking around. But in any case, Madison was certain of one thing.

If she wanted to keep it real, Madison needed to give Ivy the benefit of the doubt, no matter what. There were so many things Madison didn't know or understand.

Mom and Dad had been right.

Some secrets were not meant to be shared. And then there were the other secrets—the ones that could be shared—and kept.

Madison would keep this one under lock and key.

Chapter 14

Madison spent her free period on Thursday in the media lab of the library. She needed to catch up on her journaling exercises from Mr. Gibbons's class.

She'd finally chosen someone for the question on point of view.

> My mother is sick and my heart is sadder than sad because

Madison stopped, read over what she'd read, and then erased the entry. For one thing, it sounded too much like her and not like the person she was writing as. Luckily she'd been writing in pencil.

She started over.

> My classmates think I'm mean. I always talk about other people, and I don't always say very nice things. They think that I think I'm the center of the universe. And most of the time, that's okay. I'm popular, I'm pretty, and I get good grades (except lately in science because Madison won't help me!).

Madison chuckled to herself but then erased the parenthetical remark. She didn't want to mention any real names.

> There are loads of things people don't know about me. And I wish people would just shut up sometimes and think about what it means to be me. Not just the part about trying to be perfect all the time (because it's hard) but the part about my mom. She is so sick. She's getting radiation treatments and she's been back to the hospital, like, four times, and my sister cries all the time. I want to cry, but it just hurts too much.

Madison stopped again, but not because she needed to erase anything. She stopped because she could see how the writing assignment was working. Mr. Gibbons and all the other English teachers in the building had assigned the journaling exercises as a way to make students dive into their writing and see the world in a richer way.

Now Madison could see.

She saw things from Ivy's side.

Some of the words Madison wrote weren't very flattering to Ivy. And some weren't even true. But when it came to the details about Mrs. Daly, Madison felt a surge of emotion that felt very real. For a fleeting moment, she imagined what it was really like to be in Ivy's world.

And it did hurt.

"What are you doing up here all by yourself, Miss Finn?" Mr. Books asked in his best whisper. He had sneaked up beside Madison while she was writing.

Madison quickly shut her composition notebook.

"Studying," she answered curtly.

"Ahhh. Working on your seventh-grade journal, I see," Mr. Books said. "Good for you. Those projects can be quite enlightening."

Madison nodded. "Mmmm."

Mr. Books walked away and left Madison alone again. After working for a while on the different-point-of-view writing assignment, she'd filled seven pages. It was more than she'd ever been able to write from her own point of view.

Although her pencil raced across the page

without stopping, Madison kept glancing up to make sure that Mr. Books wasn't spying anymore. She also kept her eyes open for signs of the enemy. The worst possible scenario would be for Ivy to come by and see Madison sitting there. What if she were to see those seven pages? Especially after she'd asked Madison to keep her mouth shut—twice?

But no one except the librarian ever approached Madison. And after finishing up the assignment, she still had time to browse through her journal just to make sure there were no parts in there that she didn't want Mr. Gibbons to see—like the "Madison Jones" scribbles, for example, or the "I hate Ivy" pages. In the end, Madison ended up crossing out a few things and even ripping out a couple of pages.

A few minutes later, the class bell rang, and Madison headed for English. She was ready—at last—to hand her journal in to Mr. Gibbons for the first time that week.

When she walked into the classroom, Madison saw a pile of black composition notebooks on top of Mr. Gibbons's desk. Some kids had plastered the covers of their notebooks with stickers, while others had simply written their names on the tops in perfect cursive letters.

"Hey, Maddie," Fiona said, coming up behind Madison.

"Hey," Madison replied. "What's up?"

"I didn't even finish yesterday's writing assignment," Fiona confessed to Madison as she placed her own notebook on the top of the pile. "I fell asleep right on top of my journal, too. Half the pages are wrinkled."

Madison giggled. "At least it looks like you spent some quality time with it," she said.

"Ha-ha," Fiona said, laughing. She headed for her seat near the back of the room.

Madison quickly shoved her own journal into the middle of one short pile. She sandwiched it in between two others so that no one would see it easily. There was no way Madison wanted to risk leaving hers out in plain view. Unlike some people, undoubtedly, she *had* written the whole truth and nothing but the truth.

At the edge of the desk, Madison's eye was caught by the shimmer of a silvery sticker depicting an illustrated bumblebee with the words QUEEN OF EVERYTHING on it. Madison was sure she knew whom that sticker—and journal—belonged to. But for the first time since the project had begun, Madison was not tempted to peek inside.

Ivy was still the enemy, but Madison understood some things about her that she hadn't really known before. As Mom and Dad had both said, whatever Ivy wrote inside her journal—true or not—was meant to stay private unless Ivy decided to share it.

And clearly, she wasn't ready. From what Madison had seen at the mall, Ivy seemed unwilling to share almost any of her feelings about her mom's illness. Was it too hard or too scary or just too messy? Madison figured it was just too messy. Someone like Ivy Daly couldn't be popular, beautiful, *and* messy. It just didn't work that way.

Meanwhile, Madison was the total opposite. Her journal was a mess: scribbles and Hart Jones doodles and crazy stories about scars—and she loved it that way. Despite all her fears to the contrary, Madison Finn did know how to keep it real. This journal, her online files, and her e-mails to Bigwheels were the proof.

After school that afternoon, Madison returned home to find a package of Chocco Rocco cookies, wrapped in a big red bow, sitting on top of the kitchen table with a note from Mom.

Hi, there, honey bear!
Took Phin over to the dog run with Aimee's mom. We're seeing a lot of each other lately! Back before 5.
It's a gorgeous afternoon—you should do your homework on the porch!
Love,
Mom
P.S.: Got some of your favorite cookies. Don't eat too many!

Madison immediately ripped open the cellophane and carefully removed two of the giant chocolate-chip cookies, stuffing a palmful of crumbs into her mouth at the same time. Then she poured herself a glass of milk. Eating these cookies with milk after school had been a special treat since kindergarten, and it never lost its appeal. Chocco Roccos were as delicious as ever now that Madison was in seventh grade.

Taking Mom's advice, Madison returned outside and plopped down onto the chair on their front porch. The sky was a beautiful, late-afternoon blue, and the air was warmer than usual for October. She didn't even need her jacket.

After taking a few bites of one of the cookies, Madison flipped open her laptop and logged on to bigfishbowl.com. Much to her surprise, her buddy list came up and showed that Bigwheels was online. Madison sent her an Insta-Message right away.

```
<MadFinn>: r u @ school?
<Bigwheels>: yup I am but I'm in
    computer LOL & u?
<MadFinn>: home on my porch :>)
<Bigwheels>: with Phin??
<MadFinn>: no just me I have some
    reading 2 do
<Bigwheels>: I have a massive essay
    due and I haven't even started
<MadFinn>: how is ur brother?
```

```
<Bigwheels>: better thanks 4 asking
<MadFinn>: I was thinking about
   evrything u said and I am totally
   blown away
<Bigwheels>: it can be hard but
   we're cool. Eddie is saying a few
   words now
<MadFinn>: he doesn't talk?
<Bigwheels>: not much. he's delayed.
   I don't know all the details. I
   should find out
<MadFinn>: I went online to find out
   information
<Bigwheels>: really?
<MadFinn>: yes I wanted to know
   about autism so u could talk 2 me
   about things
<Bigwheels>: you did?
<MadFinn>: I'm sorry it's so hard
<Bigwheels>: thanx soooo much
<MadFinn>: has n e one told u 2day
   that ur GREAT?
<Bigwheels>: ">) ur the great one
```

As Madison sat on the porch chatting online with Bigwheels, the sun began to slip lower in the sky. The clouds took over.

Madison said her good-byes and closed the laptop. She and Bigwheels promised to talk more regularly about Eddie and school and everything. They

164

didn't want to keep anything important a secret.

As the sky got darker, the air got cooler. Madison shut her laptop and wrapped her sweater tightly around her middle. When she had last checked her laptop clock it had been almost five o'clock. She expected Mom and Phin to pull into the driveway any minute.

In the fading light, Madison spotted a boy walking down the sidewalk. She didn't recognize him at first, but as he came closer she realized she knew *exactly* who it was!

Hart?

"Finnster!" Hart lifted his hand and waved as he approached.

Madison leaped up from the chair where she'd been sitting. She placed her laptop onto a small table.

"Hart!" Madison cried. "What are you doing here?"

"I was over at Chet's," Hart said, sounding a little out of breath. He'd jogged the last few yards to Madison's porch steps. "We were playing Disaster Zone again. But without Egg. Chet and I have decided that we're going to challenge him to a game and beat him. He always thinks he's the king of video games, but I want to prove him wrong."

"Sounds good to me," Madison chuckled. "Anything to make Egg eat his words. Ha!"

"Where's Phin, your dog?" Hart asked.

"With my mom," Madison said. "They went to the store."

"So you're alone?" Hart asked.

"Just doing some surfing online," Madison said. "Um . . . you want to sit down for a minute?"

Madison knew that Hart would accept her offer. After all, if he'd been over at Chet and Fiona's house, he had probably been planning to take the bus home. The route to the bus didn't go past Madison's house—it went in the opposite direction. Passing by 5 Blueberry Street was a planned detour.

Sure enough, Hart sat down in the chair next to Madison.

"You have something on your chin," Hart said, pointing to his own chin to indicate the spot.

Madison reached up and brushed off a huge cookie crumb.

How embarrassing.

"My mom left me some Chocco Roccos," Madison said. She pointed to the extra cookie she'd left on the table. "Want one?"

"Oh, yeah," Hart declared. "I love them! They're my favorite."

Madison grinned.

They even liked the same cookies. This had to be destiny.

After a few moments of silence, and more cookie-crunching, Hart spoke up. "So," he said, "what's new?"

"New?" Madison repeated. "I turned in my journal to Mr. Gibbons today."

"Me, too," Hart said. "Anything else going on?"

Madison looked out at the darkness that had moved in. Night was really falling. The Finns' porch light came on automatically, and Hart's face was flooded with yellow. He looked cute even in bad lighting.

Madison repeated the question. "Anything new?"

"What's up with you?" Hart asked. "You okay?"

Madison laughed. "Sure. Yeah. Of course."

"Really? Because you seem . . . well . . . you seem a little weird."

"Weird?"

"I don't mean that in a bad way," Hart tried to explain.

"Oh?"

"No, I was just wondering," Hart gulped. Madison could see his Adam's apple move. Was he nervous? She was.

"Thanks for worrying," Madison said. "But I'm fine."

"Okay," Hart said.

"Wait!" Madison spoke up. "No! That's a lie. I'm not totally fine. You're right. . . . I *have* been acting and feeling a little weird in the past few weeks."

Madison proceeded to explain to Hart everything that had happened with Bigwheels and with Mom.

167

She was tempted to tell him all about Ivy and Ivy's mom, but she didn't do that. She couldn't do that. Promises counted, even when you made them to the enemy.

Hart listened as Madison talked. And they really talked, not like at school, when everyone was together and trying to be funny or clever all the time. They talked about their parents and their feelings about seventh grade. It was almost twenty after five and Mom still hadn't come home. Madison was very grateful for that. It was like destiny.

"You know, Finnster, you're really nice," Hart said, out of the blue.

It took Madison by surprise, even though they'd been talking so honestly for almost half an hour.

"So are you," Madison admitted. It was the closest she'd ever come to telling Hart that she had a crush on him.

Hart laughed. "I feel like such a dork," he said.

There was a long silence. Well, it was probably only twenty seconds or so, but it felt like an eternity.

"We should do something," Madison blurted out.

"Yeah?" Hart said with a smile.

But then Madison sighed.

"What?" Hart asked.

"Well, you already asked me to the movies once."

"I did?" Hart said, playing dumb.

"Oh, don't you remember?" Madison said. "It

was with everyone else at the mall, and I thought that it was sort of like . . ."

"Finnster, of course I remember asking you," Hart said. "And we went, didn't we?"

"Sort of," Madison said. "Although I'm not sure if we talked much."

"Not like now," Hart said.

"No," Madison said. A warm breeze blew, but Madison shivered. This was one of those moments she'd been waiting for—forever.

Sunset. Porch. Alone. *Hart.*

"So . . . we *should* do something," Hart said. "I mean, is it okay if I ask again?"

"Want to go to the movies again with everyone?" Madison asked.

"Sure. Or something else," Hart said.

"That would be cool," Madison said. She felt a little light-headed as they sat there, and one of her biggest dreams unfolded before her very eyes. It was like one of those moments from a romance movie. Madison glanced over at Hart's hand. His fingers were tapping the arm of the chair.

Did he want to hold hands? Madison wished she were sitting a little closer so she could find out. After all, he *had* grabbed her hand just the other day (although Madison knew that that hadn't really been a romantic grab).

"You know," Hart said slowly. "I should tell you something."

"What?" Madison asked. Her face was flushed with anticipation. This really *was* a scene from a movie.

"Well, do you remember the day when you and I collided at school? And your bag fell apart?"

Madison did remember. "Yeah?" she asked tentatively.

"Well . . . I saw your journal that day. I saw what you wrote."

Madison had never felt her stomach flip and then flop more than it did at that moment. "You saw?" she asked.

"I saw my name on the page."

Madison could hardly keep herself from running—*screaming*—from that porch. Her feet wanted to go, her head wanted to go. *She* wanted to go! *He had seen it?*

She'd been staring at Hart in wonder. Now she couldn't even glance over at him.

"I think I'm going to be sick," Madison said.

"Don't be embarrassed," Hart said with a little chuckle.

Is he laughing at me now? HELP!

"It was stupid," Madison said quickly. "What I wrote. I was just goofing around. I'm sorry."

Just then, bright headlights shone. The porch was flooded with light as Mom pulled into the driveway.

"Your mom's home," Hart said. "I guess I should go."

"Yeah," Madison said, standing up. "I guess."

Mom unloaded Phin from the car first. She waved to Madison and Hart. Phin raced over and jumped right up onto Hart's leg.

"So we'll do something," Hart said as he started for the porch steps. He patted Phin's head. "Later, Finnster."

"Later," Madison said.

Madison watched as Hart gave Mom a friendly hello and then disappeared around the hedge.

Mom walked over to Madison. "What was *that* all about?" she asked.

"Oh, he was just walking by," Madison said.

"Hart Jones was *just* walking by? Oh, Madison, he likes you," Mom said.

Madison broke out into a wide grin.

"I know," she said, believing in her heart, at last, that things between her and her crush were realer than real.

171

Mad Chat Words

LTNE	Long Time No E-mail
Kewlest	Coolest
WTP	What's the point?
HW	Homework
BFB	Bloggerfishbowl
ESP	Extra Sensory Perception
*>)	Keep a secret (or, wink)
Un42n8ly	Unfortunately
Ppl	People
ATT	All the time
)?	My brain's empty! Huh?
:*;	Big sniffle
JSS	Just so sorry
JSS2	Just so sorry, too

Madison's Computer Tip

When I discovered Bigwheels's blog on BLOGGER-FISHBOWL, I panicked. I couldn't believe that one of my closest friends (and my very best online friend) would have kept a computer diary without telling me. But she did. It hurt my feelings. But soon, Bigwheels had to tell me about what was really going on. She realized that by keeping a blog, she exposed her thoughts and feelings to everyone, including me. **If you want to keep your thoughts and feelings secret, don't write them down in a blog.** Everything you write online will likely get seen my someone else. I don't think I'm ready to turn my files into a blog. I like keeping some of my thoughts and feelings private—especially the ones about Hart.

Visit Madison at www.madisonfinn.com